WHEN RUFF JUSTICE WOKE, SHE WAS STANDING THERE, NAKED. . . .

At the bedside was a tray of food.

"Hope you didn't go out like that to fetch those vittles."

"No," she laughed. "Would that bother you?"

"Of course. Every man is jealous, but I'm especially jealous of you just now."

"Yes," she said, smiling, "I'll bet."

"What's to eat?"

"Have a look. It doesn't bother you if I sit around like this, does it?"

"Not a bit. It's a little distracting, but I'll manage."

He did manage. He managed through four eggs and two thick slices of ham, grits, potatoes, and coffee. Then he couldn't manage anymore and he threw off the sheets and, smiling, she came to him again, searching his body with fingers and lips. . . .

RUFF JUSTICE #13:

POWDER LODE

by

Warren T. Longtree

A SIGNET BOOK
NEW AMERICAN LIBRARY

PUBLISHER'S NOTE

This novel is a work of fiction. Names, characters, places, and incidents either are the product of the author's imagination or are used fictitiously, and any resemblance to actual persons, living or dead, events, or locales is entirely coincidental.

NAL BOOKS ARE AVAILABLE AT QUANTITY DISCOUNTS WHEN USED TO PROMOTE PRODUCTS OR SERVICES. FOR INFORMATION PLEASE WRITE TO PREMIUM MARKETING DIVISION, NEW AMERICAN LIBRARY, 1633 BROADWAY, NEW YORK, NEW YORK 10019.

The first chapter of this book appeared in *Petticoat Express*, the twelfth volume of this series.

SIGNET TRADEMARK REG. U.S. PAT. OFF. AND FOREIGN COUNTRIES
REGISTERED TRADEMARK—MARCA REGISTRADA
HECHO EN CHICAGO, U.S.A.

SIGNET, SIGNET CLASSIC, MENTOR, PLUME, MERIDIAN AND NAL BOOKS are published by New American Library,
1633 Broadway, New York, New York 10019

First Printing, April, 1984

1 2 3 4 5 6 7 8 9

PRINTED IN THE UNITED STATES OF AMERICA

RUFF JUSTICE

He knew the West better than any man alive—a hostile, savage land rife with both violent outlaws and courageous adventurers. But Ruff Justice had a sixth sense that kept him breathing and saw his enemies dead. A scout for the U.S. Cavalry, he was paid to protect the public, and nobody was faster at sniffing out a killer, a crook, a con man—red or white, at close range or far. Anyone on the wrong side of the law would have to reckon with the menace of Ruff's murderously sharp stag-handled bowie knife, with his Colt pistol, and the Spencer rifle he cradled in his arms.

Ruff Justice, gentleman and frontier philosopher—good men respected him, bad men feared him, and women, good and bad, wanted him with all the wildness of the Old West.

1

There couldn't have been more than three of them in the cabin below the bluff. Three outlaws left from the Morgan gang, which had stormed into Bismarck six days earlier and tried to open up the bank. Five of them had been left dead in the streets. Armed irate citizens had objected strenuously to losing next year's seed money, the nickels put painstakingly away to buy a new mail-order corset.

Five dead in the streets of Bismarck and three townspeople, including the banker and a twelve-year-old kid. Marshal Shearer hadn't wasted any time. With ten men behind him he had ridden directly to neighboring Fort Lincoln and marched himself into the commanding officer's office.

"The Morgan gang just hit the bank," Shearer said, leaning across Colonel MacEnroe's desk. "I want you to give me a dozen men to go after them."

It wasn't a good way to approach MacEnroe. The colonel's color darkened and he narrowed his eyes. "It's not up to us to provide you with a posse, Shearer, and you know it."

"Damn you, MacEnroe, this is your town too. I've got a twelve-year-old boy dead and the Morgan gang making a run for the foothills. They've got our money, they've killed our people."

"You've got no one in town who'll ride with you?"

"I've got ten men right now. It won't be enough. Once we get out into Indian country, they're going to get almighty shy. They won't stick it out."

"Then they don't much deserve to get their money back, do they?"

"If we had soldiers with us . . ."

"I don't have any soldiers to spare, Shearer!" MacEnroe rose behind his desk. He was a tall, imposing man with a silver moustache. He was annoyed with Shearer—sorry for him, but annoyed nontheless. "I've got Captain Markham up near the Canuck line chasing down that animal Sky Warrior; I've got Lieutenant Cooper out with two platoons on the western perimeter trying to locate that Sioux force that is drifting along the Heart. That leaves me one officer and three platoons. That officer is Lieutenant Harkness, who just came in yesterday from three weeks in the field; he took an arrow in the thigh. I'm sorry for you, Shearer, I'd like to help, but I can't strip this post for you. No, I don't have anyone."

"All right." Shearer stiffened, his mouth compressing into a tight line. "If that's the way it's going to be. Just don't you forget that you've turned your back on the people of Bismarck . . ."

"For Christ's sake, Shearer, shut up."

"Yeah, I'll shut up." The marshal mopped his forehead with a red handkerchief. "Listen, MacEnroe, I've got myself a situation. I'm not a bad town marshal. I think people will tell you that, but I'm not cut out for that wild country. If you could give me a hand—like an Indian scout, maybe." Shearer looked worried now, more concerned than angry. He had a town depending on him.

"They're all out," MacEnroe said. "Except for one who just came in with Lieutenant Harkness, but he's due some leave and I don't think he'd want to ride out with you. He was leaving for Denver. You can ask him," the colonel added.

MacEnroe was looking beyond Shearer, and it was only then that the marshal realized there was another man in the room, sitting in a wooden chair against the wall. He was a lanky man with long dark hair that curled down past his shoulders; he wore his moustache drooping to the jawline. He had icy blue eyes, a somewhat narrow nose, a mocking mouth. He wore a gray suit just now, and his black boots were highly polished. On his knee was a new white stetson with a low crown. His shirt had ruffles down the front. Someone less observant, less knowing, might have taken him for a dandy, but Shearer had been around some. He knew the look in those eyes. He thought he knew the name.

"Ruffin T. Justice?"

"Yes. I hear you've got a little problem."

"I've got myself a large problem, Mister Justice. And I guess I made a fool out of myself by not coming in here and admitting it. I need a scout, and need one bad. The Morgan gang's got a good start and they've got good horses under them. I hear you're on your way to Denver. I shouldn't ask you to delay your trip, but if you could possibly help us, I'd be forever grateful. So would all of Bismarck."

Ruff smiled thinly. He didn't believe in eternal gratitude. "A twelve-year-old was killed. Who got him?"

"They say Rufus Morgan. And it wasn't no accident. It was Hugh Thomas' kid, the blacksmith. He had a squirrel gun and tried to stop them."

"I'll change my clothes," Justice said. He exchanged a glance with Colonel MacEnroe. "Fifteen minutes."

In fifteen minutes Ruff Justice was leading the posse out onto the Dakota plains. He wore fringed buckskins, a gun belt that held a Colt revolver and a back-slung, razor-edged Bowie, and he carried a buckskin-sheathed Spencer .56 rifle.

Colonel MacEnroe stood on the plankwalk before the orderly room with his massive first sergeant, Mack Pierce, beside him. Both men squinted into the harsh sunlight, watching the horsemen.

"I don't think I'll ever be able to figure that man out," MacEnroe said, meaning Justice. "He's been badgering me for months to let him go to Denver."

"I read him," Pierce said slowly. "He knew the kid, you know."

"The Thomas kid?"

"Yes, sir. He knew him. He used to take him fishing with him. It's personal, Colonel. It's personal and I can damn near pity Rufus Morgan for what he's got coming now."

Ruff Justice was pressed against the rim of the bluff, looking down upon the shanty where Rufus Morgan and two of his men had taken refuge. The sun was dropping lower, glinting orange through the willows along the river beyond the shack.

Justice felt the sweat trickle down his cheeks and throat, felt the prickly heat on his flesh. His mouth was dry, his eyes hard and cold. The Colt was clenched, thumb hooked around the curved hammer, in his right hand.

There were three outlaws below, only three. Of the posse, there was only Ruff. Six men had turned back the second day after the Indian sign became prolific. A hundred Sioux warriors had crossed their trail only the day before, and the townsmen didn't have the heart to continue.

"Let the Morgans have the money. They won't live long enough to spend it."

On the following morning they had run right into the outlaws, almost literally. The Morgan gang, believing themselves safe from pursuit, had been late in breaking camp, and the posse burst through the trees practically on top of them.

Three outlaws had gone down in the first barrage. A horse had cried out with pain; Marshal Shearer, holding his shattered thigh, had been thrown to the ground. Five of the Morgan gang had plunged their horses into the river. Bullets from Ruff Justice's big .56 repeater had stopped two of them before they had reached the far bank.

There were only two of the posse left alive. Shearer and a cowboy named Wright. But Shearer didn't look like he was going to last long. The color had washed out of his face. He was sitting propped up against a fallen cottonwood when Ruff returned, Wright trying to stem the flow of blood from a jagged wound.

"That's done us, I guess," Shearer said.

Ruff smiled. "Done you anyway, Marshal." Justice had helped splint the leg. They couldn't do much about the bleeding.

"Maybe if we get him back to town, he'll make it," Wright had suggested.

"Maybe." The kid looked anxious to get himself back to town. "That's all there is to do. We can rig up a travois maybe."

"Justice!" It was Shearer who spoke, his voice weak and dusty. "We can't let them get away."

"We won't."

"I won't go back to town."

"You'll have to, I'm afraid. Don't fret. I'll get them. Every single one."

"You're going on alone?" Wright asked in disbelief.

"Oh, yes." Justice stood looking across the glimmering river. "I'm going after them." Then he helped Wright fashion a travois out of two long willow poles and a saddle blanket. When he had last seen Shearer, the marshal had been unconscious, tied to the travois, jouncing back toward Bismarck.

Ruff tensed—the door of the shack below had opened a bare inch. Someone was peering out. He would see nothing. Justice was out of the line of sight, fifty feet above the cabin on a sandy bluff, a hundred feet away. The door closed again. They would wait until dark, undoubtedly.

Fine. That suited Justice.

He lay there staring at the cabin, the glare of late sunlight in his eyes. A red ant crawled across his gun hand, but Justice didn't move.

Only the eyes moved . . . eyes that restlessly searched the land, returning periodically to the cabin. He hadn't forgotten the Sioux sign. They were out there as well. Perhaps the gunfire had chased them off; perhaps it had drawn them nearer, piquing their curiosity.

The sun had dropped another degree or two, the orange rim of it disappearing behind the willows. Still Justice held his position. He could see movement in the trees behind the shack: a hobbled horse restlessly moving around.

The breeze rose at sunset, cooling Ruff's heated flesh. The dove winged homeward and the night birds began to appear. An owl swooped low, following the river as it searched for insects.

The first star blinked on, shining through the orange haze of sunset, and Justice began to move slowly from the bluff, backing down toward his horse, bringing a stream of sand with him.

He left the horse, circling on foot through the catclaw and sage, the willows toward the trees behind the shack. The outlaws were going nowhere without those horses.

If Ruff Justice had his way, they were going nowhere at all.

He came up slowly, silently, on the horses, not

wishing to startle them. A roan lifted its head and began to quiver as if it would whicker, but it did not. Perhaps it was just too weary. Some of the horses still wore saddles. All of them were sweat-streaked, beaten. The outlaws had ridden them hard.

To one side, seen dimly through the shadows the stars cast beneath the willows, was a very tall chestnut gelding. Saddleless, it alone looked fresh.

Justice had only a moment to glance at the chestnut before he heard a twig crack under someone's boot. The sound was loud in the night. Ruff's eyes shifted that way, toward the cabin. The outlaws were coming out.

Justice hunkered down, the big Colt in his hand, and sat watching. It was time for Rufus Morgan to pay.

The first man entered the thicket cautiously. The starlight glinted in his eyes. He wore a leather jacket, jeans, a red scarf. The outlaw looked around cautiously, moving forward on tiptoes into the thicket where the horses were picketed. But he was no woodsman. He never saw the tall man in buckskins.

Justice still waited, and in another minute two more men appeared, each carrying a canvas sack.

The bearded man was Rufus Morgan. Justice's Colt automatically shifted that way. Morgan was the first target. He waited until they had assured themselves that no one was there, and when Morgan was busy tying the sack onto his saddle, his hands busy, Justice rose and took three silent steps forward.

"This is it, Morgan. Judgment day."

Morgan flinched but did not turn around. The man in the leather jacket did. He flung himself aside, grabbing for his holstered pistol. He fired wildly at Ruff from the ground. Two rapid shots sang past Ruff's head, the pistol spitting flame. Ruff's big Colt spoke in reply and he saw the outlaw buck from the impact of the .44 bullet.

Ruff dropped to a knee and turned back toward Morgan, but he was gone! The big man had taken to the brush, leaving the third outlaw to fend for himself.

"You can go back to Bismarck," Ruff said, moving toward the outlaw, who looked very young.

"And get hung?"

"I reckon," Ruff answered quietly.

"What the hell's the percentage there?"

"You've always got a chance with a jury," Ruff said. His eyes restlessly searched the willows beyond the kid. Where was Rufus Morgan? Had he taken to his heels, or was he circling back? There was little time to fool with the kid. He had to decide now where he wanted to do his dying.

"What's it going to be?" Ruff asked him.

"I've got more chance with you than with a hanging jury," the young outlaw said. Then he drew his gun.

He was wrong: he would have had much more chance with a jury. He was young and scared and desperate. His gun spewed flame and lead, but he wasn't even close in his haste. Justice answered his fire with one heart shot. The kid went to his knees, already dead, although his eyes were still open, his mouth still working.

Justice stood there in the darkness for a minute, the rolling echoes dying away, the scent of burned powder still in his nostrils, acrid, smelling of death and the promise of death.

He heard something—the slightest of sounds, a whispery movement to his right—and he backed out of the thicket, circling left, a shadowy, substanceless thing as he moved toward the sound.

The stars were bright and blue now through the lace of the intertwined willow branches. Far off, a coyote howled. The wind rustled the leaves of the willows and was silent.

Ruff was nearer the river now. He could smell it in the night, hear the tinkling of water over stones. And ahead something moving that was not water.

"Morgan," Justice said quietly, "you can't win this game. Let's go on back."

The answer was the near bellowing of a large-caliber rifle, and Justice flung himself to the earth as a bullet cut willow brush over his head.

He was on his belly, and wriggling forward on elbows and knees, he reached a small cut that led down to the narrow river. Ruff was over it and down in seconds, then running south, wanting to get back to the thicket where the horses were kept. Morgan had no chance without the horses, and he was smart enough to know it.

Panting, Justice clambered up the bank, stifling a grunt as his knee knocked against an unseen rock in the darkness. Then he was into the trees again, moving like a ghost toward the thicket, his sense of direction leading him unerringly to it.

The skies were lighter now, and as he glanced across his shoulder, he saw the rim of the moon, orange, huge, appearing above the dark Dakota horizon.

He saw the horse move in the thicket, saw simultaneously the man mounted on its back, and he fired as the rifle spoke again. Justice had missed, but he didn't miss the second time, and as the thicket was lighted by the yellow-red muzzle flash, the gurgling scream split the night. The horse went to hind legs, whinnying shrilly, and Rufus Morgan slid from its back to thump against the earth and lie there, still and dead, dark blood pouring from a savage wound at the base of his throat.

Ruff glanced at the outlaw and moved toward the horse, untying one of the canvas sacks, which proved to hold bank notes in various denominations and a quantity of newly minted gold coins.

Justice found the second sack and shouldered it as well. With extreme caution he moved toward the cabin; they had believed there were only three outlaws left, and those three were accounted for, but men had been killed by assuming too much.

Besides, the Sioux were around still. They could use that gold as well as anyone else.

The moon was rising higher, becoming round and golden. Justice reached the cabin and, approaching it silently, opened the door. He went in, leading with the muzzle of his Colt, but the place was empty.

There was a jug of corn liquor on the table, a few tins of beans, half-eaten, the scent of tobacco. In the corner were empty mail sacks, a broken shotgun, a bit of harness, a rusted shovel and pick, rags, and bottles.

Justice dropped the canvas moneybags he held and sat down, his back to the table, reloading his pistol, watching the moon glimmer on the river through the open door of the shack.

His hand, he noticed, was trembling slightly. Justice smiled thinly, rose, and holstered his pistol. He poked around the shack a little, moving the mailbags in the corner. They were all empty. In the fireplace was a heaped pile of fine ash. Paper had been burned in it. The mail, undoubtedly, had been searched for valuables and then tossed away.

Ruff took one of the empty mailbags with him and went back out. The night had grown chilly. A ground fog crept across the river toward him.

Morgan and his friends were still there, growing slowly cold, slowly stiff, nothing but a memory and a heap of bones. Justice crouched beside Morgan's body and searched it, coming up with a buckskin sack full of ten-dollar gold pieces. In an inside vest pocket were three pieces of mail, which Justice stuffed into the saddlebags on one of the horses.

A search of the other two outlaws yielded one pocket watch and two more sacks of gold. Justice left the men there, unburied, unmourned, and leading the horses, he started slowly back toward Fort Lincoln as the pale moon rose higher above the empty land. Behind him the coyotes yipped excitedly as they crept nearer the dead objects lying in the willows.

2

"Forty-two dollars short," the banker said, shaking his head. For a man who had had none of his twelve thousand an hour earlier, he seemed irrationally angry. Maybe he felt guilty. Wilburn Crandall had been head teller, the man who had meekly handed the cash over to the Morgans. The manager, a man named Phipps, had been at lunch. It was Phipps who had tried to stop the gang and been shot down.

"You're sure of that?" Justice asked.

Crandall glowered. The lean man in buckskins had trail dust on him still. His dark hair was plastered to his skull. They called him Ruff Justice, and it was he who had sauntered into the bank at ten that morning and plopped the moneybags on the counter.

"I'm sure," Crandall said, mopping his bald head with a handkerchief. "There are the books. If you would like to count it yourself, Mr. Justice . . ."

"Easy, Wilburn." It was Ned Stokes who spoke. The deputy chief marshal of Bismarck was young, gangly, and dark. Part Cherokee, Ruff guessed. No one knew if Shearer were going to recover from his wounds yet. In the meantime Stokes had taken over.

Justice had come into his office with the money, the empty mail sack, and the report that Rufus Morgan wouldn't be bothering anyone else in Dakota. Together they had walked to the bank and waited patiently while Crandall, seeming less than pleased, counted the money. Three times.

"If you're worried about the reward, Mr. Justice . . ."

"I was worried about a missing thousand dollars," Justice said, holding back his anger.

"I don't understand you."

"The Morgans should have had even more money."

"I don't see why you believe that," Crandall said a little testily.

"I'm sure Crandall knows how much the bank was missing, Justice," Stokes put in.

"Yes, I'm sure he does." Justice recrossed his long legs. "I was hoping some extra would turn up. I suppose Morgan spent the difference."

The thousand dollars that worried Ruff Justice were mentioned in the letter he had in his shirt. On the long ride back to Bismarck he had taken the time to read the three letters taken from the outlaw's body. This one had been addressed to Miss Amy Settle, Bear Fork, Dakota Territory.

Dear Amy,

Well, I am alarmed to hear of all that has happened and of your pa. I know it must be hard for a young woman alone away out there.

The thousand is rightfully yours, of course, but it is about all we got left with the drought and all. Nevertheless, it is yours to ask for and you will find the same enclosed. Also the mail rider has agreed to bring the long runner along. I don't know what use you have for the old horse, but you say you want him to and so he is before your eyes as you read this—hopefully. With best wishes,

Samuel Settle.

Justice had shown the letter to Stokes, who told him, "Sam Settle had a brother out toward Bear Fork.

Yes, I know Sam. He's given it up now. He was trying to grow wheat out here and everyone knows Dakota ain't wheat country—or maybe it will be someday, but it just isn't now. Sam has pulled out, maybe three weeks ago. I don't know where he's gone—east, he said. That's all, just east."

"Three weeks ago? When did the mail leave?"

"It's been a couple of weeks now. It piles up over at the post office for months until Blakely can find some fool crazy enough to ride that Indian country through to Bear Fork. Now, the long runner, that refers to that damned old chestnut gelding you brought in. Sam had him and always called him that. 'Damned long runner broke down the fence again,' I've heard him say. That's all I know of that family and of Sam Settle."

A fly droned over the banker's head and he swatted ineffectually at it. Justice took a slow deep breath and rose. "I don't suppose that reward would be anything like a thousand dollars."

"I don't suppose so," Crandall replied with a slight smile. "Anyway, that's got to go up to Fargo to the directors and be decided on there. It'll be some time before I can let you know what they've decided."

"All right." Justice rose. "Then that's all there is to be done here. We'll let you get back to work." He planted his wide white hat on his head and shook the banker's soft, pink hand.

Outside, Stokes said, "The man means well. He's jumpy, kind of overwhelmed with the sudden responsibility, you might say. How about some breakfast, Justice?"

"Nothing could sound better," Ruff agreed.

Together they walked down the plankwalk toward the Dutch Restaurant on Front Street. Ruff was distracted, thinking about a young woman somewhere whose father had had an accident or died, who was counting on receiving a thousand dollars from her uncle. A thousand dollars that had dried up and blown away, been lost at a faro table or given to women . . .

"Don't walk by it, Justice," Stokes said, and Ruff looked up to see that he had nearly done so. Stokes held open the door to the restaurant and the two men went inside.

The Dutch Restaurant was cool, quiet, neat. They sat at a corner table, placing their hats on the bench beside them.

"What'll it be, Ned?" the stout blond waitress asked.

"Two of everything," Stokes said. "A lot of coffee, Mable."

Justice was still preoccupied. "The mail won't be going to Bear Fork for a time, I take it."

"Not likely. You know the Sioux situation, probably better than I do. It'll wait until another man as foolish or as desperate as Bill Spears shows up."

"Spears? He was the last mail rider?"

"He was. It looks like the Morgan gang got him. Folks will know that as they know the Sioux are riding south. It'll be tough to get anyone to risk his neck for a few dollars."

"Yes." Ruff moved his elbows as the waitress came back with two platters heaped high with scrambled eggs, potatoes, grits, ham, and toast. She placed a quart granite coffeepot down, set them each up with a cup, and left, leaving them to dig in.

Ruff ate silently for a time, then asked, "What do you know about this Harlan Busby business?"

"Not much," Stokes said around a mouthful of food. "Just what the posters said when they were still looking for him. 'Wanted for murder' and a description. I heard it was some kind of fuss between two miners over to Bear Fork—or maybe I haven't even got that straight. By the time we had the posters I guess they had corralled him anyway. Said to be found in a dry well in his own backyard. His wife lowered his vittles in a bucket every day and some sharp-eyed neighbor reported it."

Ruff nodded. He dipped into his shirt, fishing the second letter from his inside pocket. "What do you think of this?"

The letter that Stokes took was undated, unsigned.

> Dear Missus Busby, they say your husband got himself a month's repreeve from the hanging. I am hopeful this letter will reach you soon enough as there is a reason I can't come back to Bear Fork personal.
>
> There is an old Mandan Indian named Fist—maybe if the sheriff there would talk to him he would find out what I already know, that your husband didn't kill Blakely at all.
>
> Sorry I'm too much fond of my own neck to return to Bear Fork and tell you this personal. I hope this letter reaches you and can help save an innocent man's neck.

Stokes finished reading the letter, reread a line again, and then handed it back to Justice with a shrug. "Maybe it means something, maybe not. I know one thing, the letter belongs in the hands of the Bear Fork sheriff."

"It's not likely to get there, is it? Not in time anyway." Justice poured himself another cup of coffee. A big-shouldered man and a young, pert-looking woman came into the restaurant, and Ruff watched them cross the room and be seated.

"Nice," Stokes commented. He poured himself a last cup of coffee and leaned back against the wall. "Look, Justice, it's a shame about Busby if he is innocent of murder—and if he's not already hung. It's too bad about the girl, too. A thousand dollars isn't that easy come by. But it don't do us any good to worry about them. The mail didn't get through and that's that."

"Yes, that's that," Ruff agreed, turning the coffeecup between his hands. "Tough for the third man, too."

"The other letter?"

"That's right. Through from Fargo . . . Well, you may as well read it too."

Stokes did. It was written on letterhead paper, FINCH-GOSSET, ASSAYERS in a slanting, cultivated hand.

> Mister Grant Danziger, Bear Fork, Dakota Territory
> Dear Mister Grant,
>
> As you know our report on your ore samples was decidedly negative regarding the productiveness of gold mining on your claim.
>
> On his own initiative one of our employees has seen fit to conduct further analysis on certain received samples, and a sense of obligation to our clients prompts this letter to advise you that you may have what proves to be an estimable pocket of copper ore in that area you have designated "C."
>
> It is our opinion that you would do well to investigate the viability of this pocket before going ahead with the sale of your property.
>
> Of course we will need further samples from said pocket to estimate cost per ton. Anticipating further serving you, we remain . . .

"That's pretty near English, isn't it?" Stokes said, putting the letter down. "This Danziger's ready to sell out a low-grade gold mine, but there's a good chance he's got a valuable pocket of copper, that right?"

"That's the way I translate it," Ruff answered.

"Tough. He'll never know."

"No." Justice rose, leaving two dollars for the waitress. The sun was high in the sky when the two men went back out onto the boardwalk to watch the wagons rolling down the dusty street.

"I appreciate what you've done," Stokes said in parting. "The town does too, I know. I'll let you know how Shearer comes along."

"Yes, do that."

"For the rest of it, Justice"—Stokes shrugged—"I wouldn't stay awake nights worrying about it. Likely it's too late to do anything for any of those Bear Fork people anyway. It's just the way things go. Like me to take those letters over to the post office? The general store's on my way."

"No." Ruff shook his head. "Thanks anyway, but I believe I'll keep them for a while."

"Whatever you say. They'd be laying out there in the brush if it wasn't for you. Luck to you, Justice. Thanks for everything."

"Sure. What about the horse?"

"The horse?" Stokes looked blank for a moment. "Oh, that chestnut—what in hell have you got in mind anyway, Justice?"

"I'd like to have the horse."

"You're going to keep it?"

"For a time."

Stokes shook his head in admiration and disbelief. "You're a crazy man, Justice. I've heard the stories, but now I know it. You're plain crazy."

Colonel MacEnroe was of the same opinion.

"I thought you were in some godawful hurry to get to Denver, Ruff. I figured there was a woman waiting."

"She'll wait a little longer. I've just changed my mind, that's all."

"It's your leave." MacEnroe shrugged. "Unless you'd be willing to postpone it for a while. Cooper's lost those Sioux he was pursuing . . ."

"No. Thank you, no," Justice said. "I believe I'll

just go ahead and ride over to Bear Fork and deliver these letters. Shouldn't take me more than a week."

"I'll look for you in two," MacEnroe growled. "I don't see what you hope to accomplish, Justice. The girl who was expecting a thousand dollars, for instance—she's not going to be real thrilled to end up with nothing but that horse. Don't expect any thanks."

Ruff smiled. "A man who expects thanks had better just not do anything, sir. Call it curiosity. Besides, it'll give me a chance to take a leisurely ride—something I don't do much."

"No, and I don't itch in red flannels. Leisurely, God, Justice, our intelligence has that entire area between here and Bear Fork, south to Belle Fourche, alive with Sioux and Cheyenne. You've got the same chance that mail rider had, you know that?"

Ruff only smiled, touched his hat brim, and walked out. MacEnroe watched him go wonderingly. The man had a funny idea of how to spend off-duty time. With Justice maybe it was congenital. Maybe he couldn't stand life without the excitement. MacEnroe had seen him take many risks, some bordering on the foolhardy.

Then again, the colonel thought as he opened the bottom desk drawer and removed the bottle of bourbon stored there, maybe Justice was just plain crazy. The colonel poured himself a stiff drink and went back to his paperwork.

Justice saddled his buckskin horse and tied a bedroll up behind the saddle. After that, he slung a sack of provisions over the pommel, checked his animal's shoes, and patted its neck.

All the time the chestnut horse standing in the next stall watched the tall man morosely. A long-jointed, long-necked, hammerheaded beast, the chestnut moved with a lazy, awkward gait. It was all of eight years old and had a cast in one eye. Ruff had seen to it that it had oats the night before, and the chestnut had picked at them with an air of one receiving its just due.

The horse was somewhat gaunt, but considering it had been running with the outlaws since the mail rider was killed, it was in decent shape.

"Ready to get back on the trail?" Ruff asked the chestnut as he slipped a lead line around its neck. The horse blew disparagingly through its nostrils.

"Goin' far, Mister Justice?" Corporal Henshaw, who was overseeing a paddock clean-up crew, asked as Ruff rode out.

"I hope so."

He hoped he was going all the way to Bear Fork and back, but it would have been tough to get decent odds that he would make it.

Ruff rode out at midmorning. The Missouri slithered away southward, silver and broad in the sunlight. Ahead, the plains were empty; the sky above was a deep, flawless blue. Justice hooked his knee around the saddlehorn and leaned back in the saddle to pass the time singing.

The first day's ride took him past the scattered, dwindling settlements. After that he saw no other human being for days, nothing but the long grass, the flowers flourishing in the hollows, and the occasional buffalo herds moving northward slowly as the days lengthened and the grass returned to the north country.

He rode warily whenever he spotted buffalo. Wherever they were, there was a chance of Indians, and he was a lone rider far from any help.

At dusk on the third day he watered his horses at the creek where the Morgan cabin had been. Ruff had seen it earlier in the afternoon. It was burned to the ground. The Sioux had no liking for the white man's fragile monuments.

"They're close around somewhere," Justice said to the buckskin. He was hunkered down on his haunches beside the horses, watching them drink, watching the river turn gold and purple in the late light, watching the late flying ducks winging their way north across red-violet skies.

The buckskin lifted its muzzle from the river and turned its head toward Ruff, water dripping like rivulets of mercury from its nose. Seeing that the man had no more to say, it got back to its drinking.

Ruff left the horses picketed near the river among the sycamores where there was good graze: bright-green young grass cropping up to replace the long dry stalks of the previous year, as attractive to horses as to the buffalo.

Justice, taking his Spencer with him, circled to a low knoll to the south and west and climbed it while sunset flushed the land, altering the perspectives of hills and valleys as they changed to orange and then deep purple, the shadows gathering in the arroyos and wallows, along the coulees to the south.

Ruff sat there in silence as the land went dark, watching his back trail, for he had that feeling upon him, a feeling he didn't like: someone was back there.

He saw no one then, nor did he see the light of a campfire when the sun had gone down beyond the western hills, and after it had been dark a full hour, Justice clambered back down, walked to check on his horses, and then ate.

He was up with the false dawn, peering at a sky flooded with waterfowl returning north. On the river, coots cried from the rushes. A four-point buck deer was drinking from the river's edge and Justice watched it for a long while until, feeling eyes upon it, the deer bounded across the river and into the wall of brush opposite.

Justice ate again—biscuits and tinned peaches, a slab of smoky jerky—and again prepared to move out. The chestnut looked at him sleepily, wearily, and Justice shook his head. The long runner looked as if it would have a tough time walking the next few miles. He had noted the numerous brands on the chestnut—frequently a sign of a troublemaker that is purchased and sold again quickly. Samuel Settle had apparently had trouble with the old hammerhead. What was it he had said to Stokes? "Damned long runner broke down the fence again."

"Onery one, are you?" Ruff asked. The chestnut didn't look it. It didn't seem to have the ambition to be onery. Its head drooped and it pulled at a patch of grass.

Ruff ran a hand along the neck of his buckskin horse and slipped the bridle on, the halter strap clicking in its buckle. He tossed the saddle over and cinched up, slipped the bit in the reluctant buckskin's mouth, buckled the throat latch, knotted the tie rope around the horse's neck, and fastened the neat coil to the saddle string.

Then, tying on his provision sack and bedroll, he moved out, the rising sun warm on his back as he splashed across the mirror-bright river, leading the sorry-looking chestnut.

He paused at the hogback ahead of him to look back down his trail once more. He had that feeling, dammit, and he didn't like it. Someone was riding in his tracks.

Who and what for? To steal that chestnut?

Maybe. If it was an Indian. To steal the chestnut, lift Ruff Justice's long dark hair, and return to the camp with a fine rifle and a Colt revolver.

Maybe.

Justice had made his share of enemies along the trail, and not all of them were buried. There was no one back there that he could see, but the feeling persisted. Ruff rode on, keeping to the high ground as much as possible here where the rolling hills met the deceptive coulees that opened up in sudden chasms beneath a horse, where an entire army of hostile Indians could, and had, hidden before an unsuspecting cavalry patrol—or a lone rider.

By noon, the sun hanging torpid and white in a pale sky, Ruff had begun to find fresh Indian sign. A party of twenty men, all mounted, most with spare ponies. No women were with them, no children, no dogs. These were a hunting party. Or a war party.

The tracks were angling southward and westward, toward the dark, low hills beyond. Toward Bear Fork. Justice stopped worrying about the phantom behind him and started concerning himself with the all-too-real Sioux ahead.

He rode with the Spencer unsheathed now, carried across the saddlebow, his eyes squinting into the glare of midday.

The still figure near the clump of cholla cactus caught his eye and he veered that way, seeing the buffalo calf dead, fly-ridden.

Still holding his rifle, Justice swung down. There was nothing left of the calf but entrails, hide, hooves, and head. He knelt down and touched its purple tongue. It was barely dry. Killed very recently, much too recently.

He started back toward his horse, moving rapidly now, uneasiness crawling up his back like a horde of small insects. The first Sioux burst from the coulee to Ruff's left, his war cry filling the air, and Justice, going to one knee, cut loose the thunder of the big .56 Spencer. He caught the warrior full in the chest, cartwheeling him from his horse's back.

That one hadn't hit the ground before two more, then three appeared, and Justice, sprinting for his horse, saw the bullets from their Winchester repeaters cut dark furrows in the earth before his racing feet.

A shot from Ruff's left turned his head that way. A

weirdly painted warrior was nearly on top of him, his pony frothing at the mouth as the Sioux raised his rifle to his shoulder and fired.

The bullet was wild; Ruff's, fired from a steadier position, wasn't. The paint pony caved in, its knees buckling as the rider was thrown free to be crushed by the rolling horse.

The animal cry of surprised pain from behind Ruff caused him to turn again, and a strangled curse rose up in his throat. The buckskin was down, kicking wildly as the blood flowed from its heart and stained its doe-colored hide.

The horse was down and the Sioux were on top of him. There wasn't a chance in the world for him. Ruff Justice turned, a savage anger welling up in his heart, and he fired the Spencer, fired it until it was empty, seeing three warriors go down in his sights. It wasn't enough. Nothing was enough. They were armed and angry, and the big .56 was silent and useless.

3

There wasn't much choice about things. Justice took three flying steps and leaped onto the back of the broken-down chestnut horse. He heeled it savagely, drawing his Colt as the chestnut lurched into ungainly motion.

The Sioux was riding directly at Ruff, and Justice saw his gun come up. Both men fired at the same time. Ruff felt the near whiff of a bullet, the burning along his neck. He paid little attention to it, however; there just wasn't time.

His own bullet must have tagged the Sioux, tagged him hard, for he was lifted from the saddle and hurled to the ground, and Ruff was free, riding across the plains. He looked behind him, seeing the buckskin dead against the ground, seeing a dozen painted warriors whipping their ponies into a streaking run.

"Move, damn you!" He heeled the chestnut beneath him again, but it did not, perhaps could not, increase its speed. It moved along at a steady, loping pace, and Ruff, glancing back, guessed that the Sioux had already closed a third of the distance.

He fired three shots from horseback, seeing one of them hit home. Fumbling with the cartridges in his gun belt, he reloaded as the chestnut jounced along over the uneven ground, heedless of all of Ruff's urging, of his hand and heels.

Without reins Justice couldn't do a thing but wrap the mane around his fingers, lean low across the withers, and watch with a sense of powerlessness the Indians closing the ground.

Their war whoops filled the air. A near bullet took a notch from the chestnut's ear. Even that didn't hurry it along. Nothing could, apparently.

The chestnut dipped into a coulee on its own initiative, and Justice clung to it as it scrambled up the sandy bank on the far side.

He had barely made it up onto the flats opposite when the first of the Indians started down the other side of the coulee—no more than thirty yards behind him.

There for a moment Ruff thought of bailing out. There was a deal of brush near the coulee, and from cover he would be able to take a few of them. In the end their numbers would triumph, however, and he stuck with the chestnut, cursing its plodding, loose-jointed pace, its heavy feet.

It was running, he would give it that, but the Sioux were gaining ground all the time. Justice cut loose three more wild shots, trying to slow the pursuit, but the Sioux had no fear on this morning. Maybe their omens had all been favorable. This night the long hair scalp would decorate their lodge.

"Like hell it will," Justice shouted wildly. He fired across his shoulder and saw a Sioux go down. An answering volley sang past him. Ahead, far ahead, were the dark hills, Bear Fork, the only settlement for miles.

He whipped the chestnut frantically with his hand, but it did no good. The horse had but one pace, and it had found it and intended to stick with it.

Yet it ran. It ran, and after the second or third mile,

Ruff realized that the Indians were no longer gaining. Their bullets still searched for flesh and bone occasionally, their shrill, yipping war cries still sounded, but they weren't gaining.

It was another mile before Ruff realized what was happening, why the Sioux were holding back. Their ponies were simply tiring. That damned, long-necked, hammerheaded chestnut was leaving them behind.

It simply loped on doggedly, its neck stretched out, its ungainly legs working like machinery. It seemed tireless, and though Ruff had never seen a horse so slow over the first mile, it was now definitely putting distance between himself and the Sioux warriors.

The Indians weren't inclined to give up, however; they pursued across the yellow-grass plains that were now studded with nopal cactus and with stunted oaks as they drew nearer the hills.

And still the long runner maintained its pace. They had gone, by Ruff's reckoning, ten or twelve miles now, and looking back once more, Justice saw that two of the Indians had pulled up. In another mile there was only one left, a vermilion-daubed warrior on a black horse. That one wouldn't be denied his scalp.

Mile after mile passed, the methodical chestnut still moving easily, not laboring at all, not breathing hard. It seemed the horse could run to the ends of the earth at that same deliberate pace.

Traces of a wagon road began to appear—deeply worn ruts in the yellow earth—and the chestnut followed them instinctively. It was even possible that the horse knew where it was. It had been in Bear Fork, after all. Maybe it was going home, eager to get there.

Ruff looked back again and he saw it happen. The black horse the Sioux was riding was foundering, but the warrior wouldn't let it stop. His hand rose and fell savagely as he whipped it—until the black simply caved in and horse and rider went down. As the chestnut loped toward the dark hills.

It was another fifteen miles to Johnstown. Ruff wouldn't have known the name of the place, but it was written large on all three of the shabby buildings there. Two were of stone, with narrow firing slots built in. The third was a log-and-mud shack that had a sloppy sign, JOHNSTOWN GENERAL STORE.

The shadows had gathered in the crotches of the dark hills. In the cottonwoods birds sang. A yellow dog trotted out to follow Ruff Justice as he walked the sweat-streaked chestnut down the trail that he supposed was Johnstown Boulevard.

It was a grubby-looking place and wouldn't be there long, but it looked pretty to Justice just then. He was weary and bruised. The spine of that chestnut had nearly cut him in half.

He swung down in front of the store, found it locked with an outside hasp, and walked stiffly across the street to the larger stone building. He could smell ham hocks and greens. From around back a hog grunted. There was a pile of bottles and rusty cans beneath the sycamore tree. Ruff looped the chestnut's lead rope around the crooked hitch rail and walked to the heavy, iron-reinforced oak door that was at ground level. The work of a craftsman, obviously not the same man who had built the store.

The door swung open before he reached it.

"Howdy. Long ride?" The man was tall, balding, slope-shouldered. He wore his galluses hanging from his pants to his knees. He had on twill trousers with the knees going, stained long-sleeved undershirt, and mule-ear boots.

"Too long a ride," Ruff said with a smile. He wiped back his hair. "Are you John?"

"How'd you know?" the man asked, pleased and baffled both.

"Lucky guess. John, I need some gear and some fixings for the horse and myself."

"Let me get the key," John said, brightening as he hooked his suspenders with his thumbs and brought them up. While John was gone, Ruff turned to look at the hills, deep in velvet shadow now, at the last glint of golden sunlight spilling through a notch a thousand feet up.

"Come right along to the store," John said, reappearing with his key and a flop hat.

"I'd like to see to the horse first before it chills."

"Sure, around back." John surveyed the horse uncertainly. Maybe he was thinking there wasn't much use in worrying about an animal like that one.

He had a pole-and-sod stable in the back. There were three other horses there, Ruff noticed. John's hay was cured, all right; his oats were a little moldy; but he made sure the chestnut had a dip anyway.

He rubbed it down carefully while the town owner forked fresh hay over from his crib. The chestnut, to show its appreciation, tried to nip Ruff's ear.

Ruff slapped its head away. "I'm grateful, but not that grateful," he growled.

The chestnut snorted and got to the oats, appearing aloof and bored, obviously feeling vastly superior to these two-legged creatures that were good only for finding oats.

There was just enough light to see. John had lit a lantern and he came back holding it up, bathing his own whiskered face in yellow-orange light.

"You all right?" John asked.

"Yes. Why?"

"You got blood caked up all down your neck and on your shirt."

Ruff touched it automatically. He had forgotten about that one, and it had been a near thing.

"Sioux or Morgan gang?" John asked as he led the way across the street to the store.

"Sioux. Party of maybe twenty of them a few miles east."

"Bastards." John spat. "They won't come around here, though, except maybe to try for one of my horses or hogs. They tried it once. Place is a regular fort and they know it."

"You've had trouble with the Morgans too?"

"They come through. Don't bother me much. I hide the old lady and let them drink."

"They won't be coming through for a while," Ruff said, holding the lantern as John fumbled with his lock.

"Do tell." His eyebrows lifted.

"They robbed the Bismarck bank. Marshal's posse ran them down."

"Somebody ought to tell Jake Morgan, then. Seen him yesterday and he was alive and kicking. Him and his brother, Art."

The door squeaked open, John lifting up on it to clear the floor. "Others are all dead, you say?"

"So the word is."

Ruff followed the storekeeper across the packed-earth floor of the cluttered general store. A pack rat scurried away at their approach.

"Hope Jake doesn't show up here for a time, then. He'll be boiling."

"Mean, is he?"

"The meanest. They were heading over to Bear Fork last I saw. You see them, you stay clear. Drunk or sober, he's mean—except he ain't sober much." A dry chuckle rose from the storekeeper's throat. "What do you want now? Saddle, bridle, bit?"

"That's right. A bedroll outfit too. Groundsheet if you got it."

"Got a nice India-rubber one. Eight by eight."

"That's big enough. I need a long gun too. Some Sioux's carrying mine tonight, I expect."

"I got a pretty used Henry, that's all."

"Forty-four?"

"That's right." John dug it out of the corner and showed it to Ruff. It was "pretty used," all right. Chipped stock, much bluing gone. The bore was worn, but it would have to do for a time.

The saddle was Texas-rigged, with a cattleman's double cinch, high cantle, and heavy pommel. It, too, had seen some use. Looking around, Ruff saw nothing that was new, now that he thought of it. He wondered just where John came up with his stock of supplies.

"There's a saddle boot I could let you have for another dollar. Might-should fit that Henry."

It did. To a T. The entire outfit, Ruff would have bet, had belonged to the same man. Maybe a cowboy gone broke. Maybe not.

"I'll tote that gear over for you later," John said amiably. "Anything else you'll be wanting?"

"Just a hot meal. Didn't I smell hocks and greens cooking?"

"You did. The old lady's got corn bread on too. We've got a couple of other gents passing through—you might of noticed their horses—and Ma's laid it out. Might be something left if we hurry on over."

"Pay you here?"

"Cash box's in the house," John said. He picked up the lantern and, smiling amiably still, led the way out.

Johnstown was dark and still. The moon wouldn't be rising for an hour. They tramped across the street and into the stone building, John blowing out the lantern as they entered.

"Ma, another plate!" he hollered as they went in.

"Set it your goddamn ownself!" a harsh voice bellowed back.

"Ma's a kidder."

"Sounds it," Ruff said. "I'll pay you, then, if you'll show me where to wash."

John looked as if he hadn't heard that word before. "Oh, well, I suppose we can set up a basin in the kitchen. Here's Ma."

Here was Ma, all right. Sloppy, slatternly, bulky. She made about two Johns. She had iron-gray hair worn in two coils over her ears. She carried a steaming platter of mustard greens and ham hocks. Small dark eyes raked John and shifted to Ruff, her frown deepening.

"He's paying, I suppose?" she demanded.

"He's paying, Ma."

"Should have said so."

She stalked off into another room. Ruff caught a glimpse of a man in a faded red shirt shoving bread and butter into his mouth before the door swung shut.

"Right over here," John said. He inclined his head toward a rickety desk. He sat in a wooden chair and pulled a rusty money box from beneath the desk. There was an open ledger book on the desk and Ruff noticed that the last entry was dated three months previous.

"I'll just tote it up now," John said, slipping out of his galluses again. "You going to want a bed too?"

"I'll sleep out," Justice said.

"Indians prowling," John reminded him.

"I can't sleep under a roof," Justice answered.

"All right . . . You know, we should have found a hat for you. Bare heads catch that sun."

"I'll make out," Ruff said, growing a little testy. "What do I owe you?"

John toted it up tediously, apparently torn between

avarice and the desire not to appear too greedy. Twice he wrote a higher figure and then scratched it out as if thinking better of it.

"Thirty-five dollars?" he said hopefully at length.

"All right."

Justice crouched down and slipped two double eagles from the inside of his buckskin boot. He kept his emergency money there, usually a hundred in gold. In the right boot his razor-edged skinning knife rode in its own hidden sheath.

He handed the man forty dollars and waited while John dug out the change, most of it in silver, which Ruff dumped into his pocket without counting.

He was shown to the kitchen and given a basin of warm water. He scrubbed his face, tenderly washed the bullet burn on his neck, and soaped and rinsed his hands. Then he walked through into the dining room and got his first good look at his fellow guests.

The man in the red shirt Ruff had glimpsed before. Tall, dirty blond, blue-eyed, with sunken cheeks and a knobby chin. The other two might have been brothers or cousins. Both dark, compact, with round faces and hands that somehow conveyed the impression of rubbery strength.

"Sit," John said cheerfully. "This here's Mister Chatsworth," he said, indicating the blond man, "and—well, I don't believe I did get you fellahs last names."

"Bob will do," one of the dark ones said. "This here's Connie." Then he got back to his eating, at which he showed considerable aptitude.

Ruff did some of the same. The food was filling, the corn bread fresh and hot. No one spoke during the meal, except that John and his wife ran through a session of bickering that seemed habitual.

"We were planning on getting up a card game, mister," John said to Ruff. "Would you be interested?"

"No." Ruff smiled. "You've got all of my money I'm going to give you."

"A little whiskey, then?"

"Don't drink, thanks," Justice said.

"Well, all right. Your gear's around to the stable. I guess we'll be seeing you for breakfast."

"I'll be gone by then. Thanks."

Ruff nodded to the woman, who only glowered back, turned, and was led to the door.

Outside, it was cool and dark, a hazy yellow moon rising up off the plains. Ruff took in several deep, satisfying breaths and walked around the corner of the gray-stone building to the stable.

The chestnut was there, saddle and bridle, bedroll and rifle.

"Let's take a little walk," Ruff said to the chestnut. He slipped the bridle on—the chestnut tried to bite his shoulder as he did so—and tossed the saddle onto the horse's back. Shouldering the rest of his gear, he led the chestnut out into the trees.

There he picketed the horse and fixed his bed. He watched the moon rise for a time, then curled up, blanket over him, Colt in hand, and slept.

It was the horse that woke him. Not by whickering, but by stamping its feet repetitively. Justice did not move as he came awake. His eyes opened slowly and he smiled almost with disgust. They were very bad at this, and he had been expecting something like it.

He could see only the one shadow. It detached itself from the trees and moved toward him, dry leaves crackling underfoot. The ratcheting of Ruff's Colt as he cocked it beneath his blanket was loud in the stillness, and the shadow halted abruptly.

"Another step, John, and I'm going to have to kill you. I told you that you had all of my money you were getting, and I meant it. I'll count about five, then you'd better be gone."

The shadow didn't hesitate. It backed up rather rapidly and was gone. The rest of the night passed peacefully.

Justice was up before dawn, smoothing his saddle blanket onto the chestnut's back, saddling, cinching up, watching the stone house where smoke rose from a chimney in the predawn.

He rode out then, noticing that the three horses were gone from the stable. That being so, Ruff decided not to follow the road into Bear Fork but to pick his way across country. He had had enough shooting to last him for a while.

4

Ruff Justice had seen Bear Fork before. He had seen it dozens of times; in the Colorado Rockies, down along the Big White River, in California. It was a mining town, or considered itself to be. It would last until the ore was played out, and then it'd be nothing more than a hundred holes in the ground, a few piles of rotting timber.

If you took three Johnstowns and put them together, you would have Bear Fork. You would have to add several saloons and a gambling house, a squat brick bank, and a second street, but the effect would have been the same.

The valley was a pretty one, or had been. Much pine timber on the dark hills that folded together and convoluted in involved, attractive patterns. A silver creek ran down from the heights where a bald mountain dominated the view.

The hills close down had been denuded and were eroded now. Smoke rose from the northern hills, probably a smelter by the sulfurous tint of it. Along one ridge was a series of shanties and tents, ramshackle shelters thrown up to keep the miners out of the worst of the weather.

Ruff heeled the chestnut, and with great reluctance it started forward and down into Bear Fork.

The sheriff's office was at the head of the street, a low stone building with a pole roof and glassless front window. Ruff tied up and went on in.

A lean, filthy man lounged behind a roughly made puncheon desk. There was a rifle on the desk and a stack of fly-spotted papers.

"Yeah?" One lazy, pouched eye opened.

"You the sheriff?"

"No."

"Where is the sheriff?"

"I'm Hawkes, I'll take any complaints."

Hawkes was making himself disagreeable. "Where's the sheriff?" Justice repeated carefully.

"Don't know. Having a drink, I expect."

Justice took a step nearer and the lean man watched him, his eyes flickering once to the rifle on the desk. "It's important," Justice went on. "At least, I hope it still is. Have you got Harlan Busby back there?"

Now the deputy's eyes definitely were on the rifle. "Maybe."

"You don't know."

Hawkes came to an upright position. His hands rested on the desk, inches from the rifle.

"Listen, my friend, I'm not here to break him out. I've never seen Harlan Busby before, but some evidence has come up that might help him." Ruff embellished a little. "Marshal Shearer over to Bismarck thought it should be delivered to the sheriff."

"What the hell kind of evidence?" Hawkes asked slowly, his eyes narrowing as he studied the tall man in buckskins. Buckskins and a scarf tied pirate-fashion over his long hair to keep some of the sun off. He looked plain dangerous was what he looked. Hawkes didn't like the feel of this. He had been having a peaceful doze, remembering a girl in Virginia, when this one came in, moving quiet and sure like a mountain cat.

"He's over at the Whiskey Well," Hawkes said after another moment's deliberation. "That's right down the street on your left. Talk to the sheriff."

"Someone mention my name?" a voice called out from the cell in the back of the office. "Someone here to see me?" All Justice could see of Harlan Busby was a pair of small hands, a smear of pale face in the shadows.

"Shut up, Harlan," Hawkes growled. "Nobody wants to see you."

The hands withdrew from the iron bars and the blur of pale face vanished.

Justice went out onto the street again. The sun was bright, but it was cooler at this elevation. He scanned the buildings up and down the rutted, corrugated street and spotted the Whiskey Well. He walked that way, leading the horse.

He hitched the chestnut outside, brushed past three men standing on the plankwalk, getting steadily drunk at ten in the morning on rotten whiskey, and walked inside the cool, dusty saloon. There were two long tables against one wall where men sat in solemn rows lifting their glasses; a pair of faro tables against another wall; a roulette wheel, which was not being used; and a rough bar. Justice walked that way, saw the star hanging on the vest front of the tall man with the unkempt sandy moustache, and halted beside him.

"You the sheriff?"

Coal-black eyes shifted to Ruff Justice. The shot glass halted halfway to the sheriff's mouth. "That's right." The shot glass resumed its trip to the lawman's lips.

"My name's Ruff Justice. Just in from Bismarck . . ."

"There he is!" The voice was strident, angry, female. "There's the man. Right dab there! Grab him, Sheriff Marks."

Justice had time to turn to look at the half-pint

female in a cotton shirt and man's jeans who was walking toward him, accusing finger leveled, before the sheriff lifted his handgun and backed away, cocking it.

"What the hell's this?" Sheriff Marks asked uncertainly. "Amy, you know there's no women allowed in saloons."

That didn't slow her down a bit. She had a torn flop hat in her hand, oversized boots on her feet. She had a mass of golden hair flying recklessly from her head, a small, cherry-colored mouth, snapping green eyes, and even white teeth. She was all of five feet tall, and all wildcat.

"I'll tell you what's going on," she said, stopping a stride away from Ruff Justice, her hands on her hips as she bent forward at the waist, her words slicing the air. "You take a walk out front, Sheriff—if you're able to, that is—and you look at the horse tied to the rail there, the horse this man rode in on, and if it's not the long runner, then by the Lord Harry, I'll stand your drinks for a year."

"You're calling him a horse thief."

"I am," she snapped.

Ruff was grinning now and she stamped a foot impatiently, not liking the lightness.

"Well?" Marks asked Justice. The Colt wavered in his hand. "You got anything to say?"

"Yes. There's a difference between riding someone else's horse and stealing it," Justice said calmly, still smiling at the young woman before him, whose cheeks had flushed to scarlet now.

"And a difference," someone interrupted, "between stealing a man's rig and using it?" The newcomer was a middle-aged man in ranch clothes. "That saddle the chestnut is wearing is sure-hell Ben Travers'. So's the rifle in the boot."

"That so?" The sheriff was growing interested.

"Anybody seen Travers lately? I haven't. Not since he rode over to Willow Bend." He prodded Ruff with the pistol. "Let's have a look."

"It's her horse," Justice said. "I was bringing it to her."

"And bringing Ben Travers his gear?"

"That I bought in Johnstown."

"Could be," someone said. "John Schick's got an almighty odd way of stocking his place, if you ask me."

"Let's have a look anyway," the sheriff said, and they went out, the girl clomping along in the lead, Justice behind her, then the sheriff and the rest of the curious bystanders.

Justice hadn't denied it was the girl's horse, but the sheriff went over it inch by inch anyway, the girl pointing out the distinguishing characteristics, the brands, the chip on its hoof, the streak of white in its tail. Ruff yawned and looked to the far hills.

"Well, look at that," Amy Settle said, "shot through the ear. Some one's shot my horse!" The chestnut decided to nip at her and she pushed its head away.

"Well, that's sure as hell Ben's saddle and gun too—Mind explaining this to me?" the sheriff asked.

"Not a bit. I'm glad you finally got around to asking," Justice said. "Can we go over to your office or do I need to make a speech out of this?"

The sheriff looked around at the gathered crowd, most of them miners, most of them with whiskey glasses in hand. "All right, let's go on over to the office," he growled.

Hawkes was still behind the desk as the three of them—Marks, Justice, and Amy Settle—tramped in. Now he got grudgingly to his feet and gave the sheriff his chair.

"Go make the rounds," the sheriff snapped at him, and the deputy, glowering at Justice as if he were responsible, snatched his hat from a peg, picked up his rifle, and went out.

"Now, then," he said to Justice from behind his desk, "what's this about?"

"It's about horse-stealin'!" Amy Settle insisted.

"You quiet yourself, Amy," the sheriff said. He showed he was no fool by adding, "It's a strange man who steals a horse, then comes looking for the sheriff. That's what this one was doing when you busted in."

"The Morgan gang," Ruff told them, "robbed and killed the mail rider a while back. He was bringing the horse and a letter for Miss Settle over to Bear Fork. I just happened to be with the posse when they took the Morgans, and I volunteered to bring the chestnut along."

"What do you do regular?"

"Army scout," Justice told him.

"And your name's Justice?"

Ruff admitted to the name. "I think we got this wrong, Miss Amy. I heard of this man. You got the letter?" he asked Ruff.

Justice fished it out of his pocket and handed it to Amy Settle. "Never heard of no thief bringing a letter along," the sheriff said.

"Why not?" She was unconvinced. "What's this prove?"

"Now, about that saddle and rig," the sheriff pursued. Justice told him how he had come by it, and the sheriff nodded thoughtfully. "Yes, I suppose that's possible. Old John, he's got his ways. Couldn't get anything on him in a hundred years, though. Just tells us someone sold him the stuff and went away. How you going to prove otherwise?"

"Where's the money?" Amy Settle cried out.

"What?"

"I said, where's the money? You look at this letter, Sheriff. Don't it say there's a thousand dollars enclosed? The money I need to keep the old place? Don't it read that way right there? Now, where's the thousand dollars?"

"Gone," was all Justice said.

"Gone where? Into some bank account in Bismarck?"

"You'd have to ask the Morgans," Justice said.

"Maybe I will—maybe I will ask Jake Morgan. And maybe I'll let him know you were one of them that killed his brother."

The girl wasn't so amusing anymore. Ruff wasn't smiling when he told her, "Lady, you've got a lot of learning and a lot of growing up to do. You're a firecracker, all right. A steamy little half-pint, but you'd better learn to listen when people talk to you."

"No man tells me what to do. Well!" She turned on the sheriff. "Are you going to lock him up or not?"

"No," Marks said finally, "I don't reckon so. I wouldn't know what for anyway."

"All right." She was panting now with the excitement. "I'll show you, Mister Justice. You'll find out you can't rob people and murder them and get away with it. Not even if the lazy drunken law lets you!"

She turned then and stamped out, jamming her hat down on her head so that it nearly covered her ears. The door banged shut and the sheriff winced as if he had the beginnings of a dandy headache.

"She does fly off. Always been that way," Marks said. "Tough on the girl since her pa died."

"How did that happen?"

"Fell. Fell from his horse. Skull was cracked wide open." Marks sighed and rubbed his eyes. "Was there something else, now, or can I get back to my business?" By which, Ruff guessed, he meant the Whiskey Well.

"There's something else." He brought the anonymous letter concerning Harlan Busby forward and gave it to the lawman, who slacked in his chair, reading it.

"This cuts no ice," he said finally. "Who wrote it?"

"I've no idea. It seemed important, so I brought it."

"It cuts no ice," the sheriff repeated. "Fist, that old Indian, I don't know where he is. He's a lying bastard anyway. All Indians are."

"You could talk to him."

"Could—didn't I say I don't know where to find him?"

"I believe you did," Ruff said dryly. "It seems you might have an idea of where to look."

"Oh, I might have an idea," Marks said, growing angry, "if I had reason to go looking. If I didn't have my duties in town. If a judge and jury hadn't already tried Harlan Busby and found him guilty of killing Blakely for his share of the claim. If I had any idea that the writer of this letter knew anything. If I knew who it was—not just some troublemaker trying to stir things up."

Ruff nodded, his lips compressing. He glanced toward the back of the jailhouse, seeing the hands wrapped around the cell bars, seeing again that blur of face.

"Mind if I talk to the prisoner?" he asked Marks.

"No." Marks calmed down. "I suppose not." He took the letter, Justice noted, and put it away carefully in his desk drawer. "Come along."

The sheriff walked him back to the cell and then withdrew a little ways. Harlan Busby peered out from behind the bars. His face was gaunt, his eyes haunted.

"Did I hear you talking about me?" Busby asked.

"Yes. That's right. Someone sent a letter to the sheriff saying that you didn't do it."

"No! God knows I didn't do it. But they're going to hang me."

"Not if you didn't murder your partner," Ruff said calmly.

"I almost wish they hadn't given me that stay of

execution. Maybe it's better to have done with it than to sit around here day and night waiting, powerless. Is anyone taking care of the old woman?" His eyes brightened. "Someone ought to see to her. She was a good wife. Christ, she even thinks I did it, but she wouldn't turn me in."

"No."

"I was living down in that well. For six days. Six days down there with the rats—I was glad when they found me."

"What happened, Busby?"

"What happened? The murder? I don't know. I was at the mine with Blakely. We'd had words—we always had words, so I was down on the first stope working alone. He was timbering up top. When I came up for air, he was dead. Lying there. Head smashed in. That's all. I sort of panicked, I guess. I took him down into the mine and rolled the body into the sulfur pit. I heard it splash. They came for me the next day. I saw them coming and went out the back and into the well."

"Who would have done it if not you?" Ruff asked.

"I don't know. I've no idea. No one was around. Are you going to try to clear me?" he asked, lifting his eyes again.

"Yes."

"See to the old woman, too, will you?"

"Sure."

"That's enough, Justice," Sheriff Marks said, and Ruff turned, leaving the little man to cling to the bars of the cell.

"You planning on doing what you told him?" the sheriff asked as they stepped outside onto the plankwalk. "Poke around and try to prove he didn't do it."

"Maybe."

"Dangerous business, you know?"

"Is it?"

"Maybe Busby did it and maybe he didn't. I tend to think he did, myself. But you've got no rights here. None that include interfering with the law. You'll remember that?"

"Sure." Ruff smiled. "I'll remember that, Sheriff. Can you tell me where I can find a man called Grant Danziger?"

"Danziger?" The sheriff's eyebrows drew together. "What in hell's he got to do with this?"

"Nothing at all that I know of. I've got a letter for him, that's all."

"Cork Creek—two miles up toward that bald mountain. He won't be welcoming you, though. Not Danziger."

"Thanks. Good day to you, then."

The sheriff looked as if he might say something else. He stood there for a moment tugging on his moustache. Then he muttered a good day and went back into his office.

Ruff stepped off the boardwalk, looking around for a stable. He needed a horse now, he supposed, and one with a quick start to it.

He started uptown, but hadn't taken three steps when a voice boomed out, "Justice!"

Ruff halted and turned slowly. The big man was walking toward him, the girl to one side and behind. "That's right. I'm Ruff Justice." He asked, "Do I know you?"

"You do now," the big man said, biting off the words. "The name's Morgan—Art Morgan."

5

Ruff stood motionless in the middle of the rutted street. A mule-drawn wagon clattered past. The sun was high and hard in a cold blue sky.

Art Morgan stood ten paces away, his bearded face twisted with liquor-born emotion. He had a pair of Colts strapped around his hips, riding low, just beneath the fingertips. The guns had been used many times.

"What's your problem, Morgan?" Ruff asked. He removed the bandanna he still had on his head and wiped his brow with it. His feet were braced nearly a yard apart.

Morgan hadn't moved nearer. He stood there trembling with rage, his face nearly purple where it showed above the shaggy beard, below the dark eyes.

"I said I was Art Morgan—I hear you killed my brother."

"Did you?" Ruff glanced at the girl, who, now that she had started this, seemed terrified. Maybe she had figured Art would throw a scare into Justice, beat him up, chase him out of town. If so, she had figured wrong. Art was in a killing mood.

"Is it so?"

"I was with a posse that chased down a pack of back-shooting murderers. If your brother was one of them, then I guess I had something to do with it."

"You son of a bitch, Justice."

Ruff hadn't seen Marks come out of his office, but he was there now, and he had a shotgun in his hand. "Art, I won't have that in the middle of Main Street. Not while I'm sheriff. This is my old ten-gauge I've got here, and it's sawed down enough to spray both of you with double-ought buckshot if you start anything."

Art was flying high enough that for a moment Justice thought the sheriff's threat wouldn't stop him, but he glanced that way, saw the evil-looking express gun, and with a deep snarl turned away. He didn't have to make a parting threat. Ruff understood him. Art Morgan would be back another time.

"Justice, damn you," Marks said, "you stir things up, don't you? Why don't you do everybody a favor and drift on out of Bear Fork?"

"Soon," Justice said. Soon wasn't good enough for the sheriff, but it was the best Justice could do.

Marks watched Art Morgan walk down the street, vanish into an alley next to the stable, and reappear a minute later to ride hell for leather up Main Street, emptying his gun into the air. Then he was gone, only the dust sifting down left to commemorate his fury, and the sheriff shook his head and headed upstreet toward the Whiskey Well, definitely needing a drink now.

Justice started in the opposite direction, striding toward Amy until she broke and ran, and then he started running himself. He caught her as she dodged into a narrow blind alley behind the bank.

Ruff grabbed her arm, spun her around, and jammed her back up against the wall. Her eyes were wide, nostrils flaring, her face pale as she peered up at him.

"Here." He stepped back and handed the girl his Colt.

"What . . . what?" She looked down at her trembling hand at the long-barreled pistol.

"Do it yourself, damn you! Don't go buy yourself a man. You've got something to do, do it yourself."

"I'm not . . ."

Her lip trembled. Her knees looked ready to buckle on her, but Ruff stayed on top of her. "You think a man's a horse thief, why, you just march up and shoot him. Doesn't matter what he says. You know what's right, don't you? You know the truth." He looked at the gun. "Bang away, lady—or stay out of my shadow."

She took a step forward, her eyes wide, unblinking, a tiny thing in that outsized shirt she wore. The gun was hanging limply at her side.

"I . . ." she managed to say, and then she collapsed into Ruff's arms and he was holding her while she gurgled and bawled and hiccuped. "I must have gone crazy . . . I don't know what I was thinking. Since Pa died. Everything's been just crazy, mister. Just crazy."

She buried her face in the hollow of his shoulder and sobbed for a while. Finally she stepped back, wiping her eyes with a knuckle.

"I'll stay out of your shadow. I promise you. I'll . . . Oh, hell! I hate crying," she said with sudden anger, and slapping Ruff's Colt into his hand, she turned and stalked up the alley and out onto the street, vanishing around the corner.

Ruff Justice stood there grinning. He walked back uptown to the stable and found himself a short-coupled little roan with three white stockings, a glossy coat, deep chest, alert brown eyes.

"How's it start?" Ruff asked the stablehand.

"Mister, that's a Texas quarter horse. It comes out

of the gate, I'll tell you. There's the backyard—take him on out and have a try."

He did. The little roan felt undersized between his knees, but when he kneed it, it jumped into motion, hitting full stride at first bounce. He ran it twice around the yard, then halted the roan, listening to its breathing, which was clear and unlabored.

He ran a hand along the smooth, glossy flank of the roan, checked the hooves, and nodded. "I'll take it."

"Won't be cheap."

"Let's talk about it," Ruff answered, and they did, agreeing after three-quarters of an hour.

As Ruff led it out, the stablehand said, "You was awful concerned about havin' a quick starter—having some trouble?"

"I've had some," Ruff answered. He had developed a strong aversion to slow-starting horses, despite the fact that the long runner had saved him in the end. Having those Sioux breathe down the back of your neck didn't do a thing for the composure.

He didn't have any trouble recovering his gear. The chestnut was gone from the sheriff's hitch rail, and Ruff's saddle and bedroll were stacked on the plankwalk.

He rigged up the roan, keeping an eye out for Art Morgan and his brother, but no one was on the streets of Bear Fork. They were at their claims, the smelters, the ore crushers, which clanked and grumbled, audible for miles, or they were in the saloons, trading the fruits of their labors for raw whiskey and tepid beer.

Ruff saw almost no one until the sheriff's deputy, Hawkes showed up ten minutes later.

"Going up into the hills?" the deputy asked in a lazy drawl.

"I expect so."

"Keep your head down."

"I intend to," Justice answered, and Hawkes smiled

briefly before turning and unlocking the sheriff's office, entering to leave Justice alone.

He swung aboard and walked the roan through the next alley, not wanting to travel the length of Main Street. Then he was following a narrow, winding trail that led up toward the bald mountain; and his thoughts, as he rode, were, oddly, on a tiny imp of a woman with fire in her eyes and a vast lonesomeness in her heart.

The bulk of the mining was to the north of town, and as Ruff rode farther south, the smell of it, the sight of it disappeared, swallowed up by the green surrounding hills once more.

He found Cork Creek and followed its winding course toward the bald mountain beyond. Danziger, apparently, was a maverick sort of man. Only he had come south of the vein; they had told Ruff that Danziger wouldn't be pleased to see him no matter what sort of word he was bringing. That alone made Justice like the man he had never seen.

Being a maverick is fine. That was what Justice himself was. Oftentimes it didn't indicate a lack of sociability, a dislike of men in general, but a need to go your own way, to think for yourself and not be stampeded along with the mass.

It meant a man did his own thinking, his own fighting, and lived his life true to his own ideals—the rest of them be damned if they didn't like it.

There was a lot of willow brush down near the creek, which gurgled and frothed over the stony stream bed. Higher up, blue spruce dominated the hills, with here and there cedar. An eagle glided slowly, peacefully past, taking an updraft to the pinnacle of the bald mountain . . . Mountain they called it around here. It wouldn't have been a sandhill in the Rockies. Perhaps five thousand feet high, maybe a shade less, it was dressed in deep blue spruce for all but the last thousand feet. There, abruptly, the mountain became utterly barren. A star-shaped cap of pale stone dominated the peak and the country for miles around. Ruff didn't know enough geology to guess, but it looked very much as if the hill had been volcanic once and the lava had risen from the hot bowels of the earth to spew out, killing all that had grown or lived there, then cooled to become a sterile dome.

The shot echoed down the canyon, and Ruff yanked the roan's head aside, heeled it, and bent low across the withers, riding it into the brush beside the trail in three quick jumps. Yes—that horse could move. It had started like a jackrabbit. But it wasn't going to outrun any bullets.

Ruff hit the brush and dismounted on the run, yanking the Henry repeater from his saddle boot.

"Just turn you around and get out of here," a voice echoed.

"Danziger?"

There was a long silence. Then, "Who's askin'?"

"My name's Ruff Justice. I'm through from Fort Lincoln. I've got a letter for you."

"No one writes to me," the voice snapped.

"I've got one written to you." Ruff was circling through the brush as he spoke, climbing up a narrow rocky ridge to achieve the pines.

"I don't believe you—Justice, whoever you are—I got no people. None that know how to write or would care to anyway."

"It's from the assayers in Fargo."

"I already got their letter." A shot was snapped off into the brush below. Ruff heard it sing off a rock face and richochet into the trees. "You're lyin'. Get off my claim."

So it was still Danziger's claim—he hadn't sold it yet. In that respect, at least, Justice had been on time. Another shot was fired from above—not so very far above now as Ruff worked through the spruce trees, their needles littering the earth, deadening his footsteps.

He saw a flash of color between trees suddenly—a blue shirt or trousers.

The voice called out again. "I didn't hit you—get on that horse and get the hell out of here!"

Justice moved in a crouch now; only thirty yards or so separated him from the sniper. He could see Danziger now, at least enough to make out a red beard, a blue-checked shirt, a kneeling posture, rifle at the shoulder.

Ruff made his move. He burst from the trees and threw a shoulder into Danziger. The miner's rifle went flying, clattering down the rocky slope below him.

Danziger was big and he was solid. As he rolled onto his back, he clouted Ruff on the ear with a work-hardened fist that set the bells to ringing. Justice tried to throw a forearm across the miner's throat to pin him down, but Danziger came up with a knee that caught him in the belly and rolled him aside.

Justice came to his knees, hair hanging in his face, and he held his Colt on Danziger's belly. The red-bearded miner got to his feet, his eyes fiery.

"Go ahead, damn you. You've figured out how to get the claim, have you? All right. Shoot. Shoot me, you bastard, that's the only way anyone will ever get it."

Ruff was on his feet now too, the hammer of the Colt drawn back. Danziger was out of his head with anger. He marched right in on Justice, his fists bunched, pine needles stuck in his beard and hair.

He bellowed and charged Justice, and there was no choice. Ruff stepped aside and clubbed down with the butt of his Colt, catching Danziger at the base of the skull, and the miner went down on his face, to stay there.

Justice stood over him for a minute, panting, then he swept back his dark hair and walked back to where he had left his rifle. The horse, bewildered, had followed him up the trail, and Justice collected the reins. Shoving the rifle away, he led the roan back up the trail and through the trees to where Danziger still lay unconscious.

He loosened his cinches and took dry biscuits and jerky from his saddlebags, lifted his canteen from the pommel, and leaned back against a tree to sit eating, watching the big miner.

He had just finished when Grant Danziger gave a moan, got to hands and knees, shaking his head, and collapsed again. The second time he made it up into a cross-legged position, and his eyes, suddenly focusing on the man in buckskins, came alert.

"Damn you . . ." the miner growled.

"Want to do it again?" Ruff asked. There was no answer and he tossed the canteen over to Danziger, who spat out a mouthful of blood and took a swallow.

"What the hell do you want?"

"I told you. I've got a letter for you." Ruff found the letter, and swallowing his last bit of dry food, he sailed the assayers' report to Danziger, who stared at it for a minute before picking it up.

He read it as Justice watched him, then read it again. Danziger looked at Ruff, threw back his head, and astonishingly roared with laughter.

"Risked your butt to bring me this, did you? Come all the way from Fort Lincoln? Why, you damned fool, I wish you'd of got yourself shot on the way. You didn't do me no favor, by bringing this."

Ruff, a little dazed, just stared at him. He still had his gun in his hand and now he said, "Do you mind if

I put this Colt away? You aren't going to shoot me, are you?"

"No." Danziger got to his feet. "I suppose not."

"I don't understand what you're telling me, you know," Justice said.

"You don't?" Danziger stood over Ruff now, hands on his hips. A trickle of blood still ran from his nostrils. "You think someone like me, who's been over the hogback and beyond the ridge a time or two, don't know what copper looks like? Hell, son, I got a regular blue hole up there—that's the copper," he added, sizing Ruff up as no miner, "big blue copper-lined hole. Hell, yes, I know it. Thing was, I didn't want anyone else to know.

"I had that assayed up once by this Finch and Gosset outfit. It came out real bad, that assay did. No gold ore worth the taking, they said. Well, in no time at all folks started leaving me alone. Hell, they seen that assay long before it ever got to me, I guarantee you that."

"You had trouble before that?"

"All kinds of damn trouble. Some with who knows who, some with men who wanted to come down here and stake up next to me, legal or not—that was when they thought I had gold and plenty of it. Had some with Bull Bromfield—that is him who's been pestering me to sell out. Bull's big owner of ninety percent of that stuff north of town. Amalgamated Mines, he calls himself, but it's just him.

"Convinced him I didn't have no gold, and my trouble stopped. I could get grub at the general store again, buy ammunition, ride down the trail without someone potshooting at me, drink my water without finding it poisoned . . . that was because Bromfield thought I didn't have a thing. You see that, son!"

Ruff could only nod his head. What was it he had told the colonel back at Fort Lincoln? "A man who expects thanks had better just not do anything." Well, he sure hadn't gotten any from Amy Settle, and all he was getting from big Grant Danziger was a dressing down.

"No, between you and some—what was it? 'employee with initiative'—I'm right back where I started from. Copper's hard to handle. Me, I couldn't afford to take it out now, not in no paying quantities, although I got good stuff. Bull Bromfield could. He'll be all over my back again, son. I'll have to live with that goddamned rifle."

"No one's seen that letter but me, Mister Danziger."

"No? How do I know that? Who saw it *before* you got your hands on it anyway? No, sir. Trouble's starting up again and, son, you brought it to me. Maybe I should have shot you," he said, and he was almost smiling. Almost, but not quite.

"Got me a hell of a headache now," Danziger said. "You want to come on up and have a look, now you've come this far?"

"If you don't mind, sure. Why not?"

"I don't suppose you're after my claim. Wouldn't be no sense in you bringing that assay report out if you was, but damn that man's initiative, whoever he was."

"Maybe he was *told* to look for copper or silver or whatever he could find." Ruff swung up on the roan and Danziger stood there, thoughtfully tugging at his beard.

"Think so?"

"Just a suggestion, I wouldn't know one way or the other."

"Well, well," Danziger said, struck by the possibility, "that's something to ponder at least—not that it matters much. Come on along. It'll be dark soon, night comes quick in these hills."

Danziger led off at a swift pace through the trees and onto a narrow stony trail that the roan didn't like much. Below, the bluff fell away for three hundred feet or more to the ragged creek bottom below. The rock here was jagged, white, limestone and outcroppings of basalt, very ancient and crumbling.

"You happen to know where a Mandan named Fist can be found?" Ruff asked.

"Fist! Damn that rascal. No, I don't know. I don't want to know. It's enough for me that he cleared out of the hills. Thievin' redskin, he is."

"He cleared out, you say."

"Yes, he did—take it easy here, there's a crevice your roan won't like—about four months back, I believe. That's when I stopped losing things around the camp."

"About the time Harlan Busby killed his partner."

Danziger halted on the trail and turned to face Ruff. "What are you after, son? Who are you?"

"Just a curious sort, I guess."

"Yes, I guess you are. Better learn to curb that." He started on again. Vines and fern grew down to the trail now, dozens of tiny rills carried water across the trail and down into the white ravine.

"It was about the time Blakely was killed," Danziger said finally. "But as to Harlan Busby doing it, I doubt it. You ever see Busby?" Ruff said he had. "Well, then, you know—Blakely was a big man, son. Hell of a lot bigger than me. Maybe the second biggest man I ever seen. Harlan Busby might of yapped at him all the time like a fox terrier, but he didn't walk up and cave Blakely's skull in. No, sir, I don't believe it."

"From behind, anyone . . ."

"Wasn't done from behind. Not many people saw the body, but I did. Front of his head caved in, big bloodless blue crater from where someone—and someone big, to my way of thinking—hit him. You thinking Fist did it?"

"Is Fist a big man?"

"Tall"—Danziger shrugged—"tall for an Indian, that

is. Wiry old skunk too. I've seen him climb crags you or I wouldn't think a goat could get up. But you didn't answer my question."

"Didn't I?" Ruff shrugged. "I don't think he did it. I don't know. What about Fist, was he that kind of man? Could he have done it?" Was that what the letter writer had been trying to convey?

"Killed him and then took to the hills—maybe. Here's home," Danziger said abruptly.

It was a narrow hanging valley with scattered cedar. There had been a number of pine trees as well, but they had been cleared, probably for mine timber and the little shack that was just visible upslope. Looking back the opposite way, Ruff could see to the foot of the canyon, clearly make out the trail he had ridden up.

"Got yourself a view, don't you?"

"Yes, and I've needed it a time or two. No one comes up on me unawares. Come along, I'll feed you. If you've been living out of your saddlebags, you can stand some grub."

Ruff saw three hobbled mules and a sturdy sorrel horse up against the rising bluff where the grass was green and long. The sun was already behind the bald mountain and shadows stained the hanging valley, stretched out of the dark hills toward the plains far away.

"Where's the mine?" Ruff asked. He could see no sign of any diggings.

"Up and away, son. You wouldn't find it wandering around."

In the cabin, which was surprisingly neat for a bachelor miner, Danziger started a pot boiling.

"A little stew I got left over. Not bad. Want to wash up? I got a basin over there in the corner."

Ruff stripped off his shirt and washed up a little, Danziger watching him. "You got some fresh bites on you," the miner commented. "And a few old ones. What was it you said you did?"

Justice told him, and that started the war stories. The conversation veered around to Indians and eventually to Fist again.

"Yes," Danziger said over stew and coffee, "he's a shifty one. Sly and almighty quiet. Like a ghost, you know. If he wanted to, he could have cut my throat many times, I guess."

"He's a loner?"

"Oh, yeah. I hear he got kicked out of his tribe—I don't know. A white man don't much understand some of what goes on among the Indians. There was something about Fist had been a medicine man or some such, and one of his spells had gone wrong. Maybe the chief's son died, or the chief . . . I dunno. Anyway, he got shown the gate, banished to the bald mountain, they say."

"He's old now."

"Too old to live out the way he does, but he manages. Spends a lot of his time lifting whatever he fancies from the mines. I told you he's been here many times, taking trifles—and sometimes valuables," Danziger said with some feeling.

"And the other mines."

"Right. All of down south here—that is to say, me; the Busby-Blakely, when there was a Busby-Blakely, before the murder; and Dan Settle's digs."

"He got a daughter?" Ruff, who knew damn well he had, asked.

"Oh, yeah. Little spitfire. Old Dan was a good man. Got throwed from his horse, cracked his skull. The girl can't make it now, I don't suppose. The old man had taken a bank loan on the place to buy some equipment. Near a thousand dollars he owes the bank, I believe."

"He had gold, then—"

"Oh, yeah. Said he had." Danziger laughed, his red beard twitching. "But then, never believe a miner, Justice. They'll lie when they don't have it and damn sure lie when they've struck it. But Settle, yeah, I believe he'd struck it. Not much other reason for borrowing money from a bank—and he must have showed them something if they were willing to loan it to him."

"Maybe," Ruff said, "that was his mistake."

6

Ruff rode out of Danziger's place at sunrise. The big man was obviously not sorry to see him go. He had enjoyed an evening's talk after the long months of seeing no one in those hills, but by morning his natural unsociability had returned. At any rate, Ruff wasn't invited back.

He rode down the long white gorge as the rising sun painted the walls of the canyon pink and violet. The little rushing creek accompanied him through the great boulders and pines.

At the road Ruff hesitated and then turned south again, away from Bear Fork.

He thought of Harlan Busby and his wife. He wasn't doing a hell of a lot to get Busby cleared of the murder charge. There wasn't anything much that could be done without Fist, and Fist, perhaps frightened by something he had seen, had vanished—gone to the bald mountain, Danziger had said. Justice's eyes lifted to the barren, desolate peak.

Six miles it was to the Busby-Blakely claim, according to Danziger, but the prospector was bad on distances. Ruff estimated he had traveled ten and still hadn't found the cutoff. He didn't know what he could hope to find there either; he was beginning to wonder why he didn't just pull up stakes and get out of this country. It was just possible to make Denver, see Lil, and get back to Lincoln on time.

There was a column of smoke rising into the sky above the spruce to the left of the trail, and Justice started that way. Someone working the Busby-Blakely?

He came out of the timber to overlook a small grassy valley. Across it, nestled in the low, folded hills was a small cabin. Squinting, Ruff could see three or four horses before the place and he started that way. He knew one of the horses intimately. The long runner was unmistakable.

He was half an hour crossing the valley, fording three tiny streams. When he pulled up before the house, he could hear the sounds of argument from inside.

"No! Now, that is it. Please just get off my property."

It was Amy Settle who was talking. A calm, deep man's voice answered her.

"I'm only trying to make things easier for you, Miss Settle. This offer is to your benefit, you know, not the bank's."

"Yes," she said sarcastically, "that's the way banks do things, isn't it? To help folks out with no thought of profit."

"Helping people out," the calm, oily voice went on, "is to our profit generally, Amy. We're all neighbors, after all."

"Forget it," the second man's voice said. This one was a great rumbling voice. "She's had her chance to make something off this hole, now she can keep her claim and be damned."

Ruff swung the door open and slipped inside to lean against the jamb. It was a moment before anyone realized he was there. The first to see him was Amy Settle. Her eyes opened wide with amazement, then were clouded with shame, and eventually settled to a sort of bewilderment.

The two men were completely dissimilar. The one with the quiet voice was tall, well-dressed, neatly barbered. The banker, Ruff guessed. The other had to be, could only be, Bull Bromfield.

He was massive, with huge hands, forearms that bulged against the sleeves of his blue silk shirt. Dark hair frothed over the top of his shirt where his thick neck ended and the barrel chest began. He had a scowling, broad face, slashed across the cheek with an old white scar. He wore a brush moustache that ran straight across his upper lip and extended for two inches on either side across his heavy cheekbones. The eyes were small, dark, but hardly unintelligent. No, there was no dullness about him, only a kind of savagery that Ruff had seldom seen in a human being.

Slowly Bull Bromfield sensed Ruff's presence and he turned to glare at the lean scout.

"Who the hell are you?"

"Just a friend of the lady's," Justice answered easily, surprising Amy Settle.

The banker, if that was who he was, now turned, looking a little flustered. His graying hair was slicked back over a narrow skull.

"I don't believe I know you," he managed to say, obviously unnerved.

"Justice. Ruffin T. Justice."

"Jack Sagan." He stuck out a hand, which Ruff took briefly. "And my friend, Mister Bromfield." And Bromfield did not stick out a hand. Ruff nodded.

"I just dropped in to see Miss Settle," Justice said lazily. "You folks go on about your business."

"We have finished our business," Amy said sharply. "I think these gentlemen are leaving now, Mister Justice."

Bull Bromfield's jaw was clenched. The great vein on his forehead was throbbing, but the banker was up to it. "Yes," Sagan said, "we were just leaving. Miss

Settle, you would do well to think over our offer. Please. Save everyone trouble."

Then, putting on his gray hat, he nodded to Justice and went out, Bull Bromfield stalking after him, dark eyes fixed on Ruff belligerently.

Justice smiled in return. He didn't turn around to watch them ride out, but stood listening to the withdrawing hoofbeats, watching Amy Settle, who was tensed, her face drawn, her small body bunched, until the horses were out of sight and hearing.

"I'm glad you stopped here," she said finally with a sharp expulsion of breath. She had been holding it in without realizing it. "But why did you?"

"Just wanted to see you," Ruff said easily.

"Is that so? I don't half-believe you."

"No?"

"No, but I'm glad you were here. Why do they do that? They wouldn't leave, just stood there bullying me. Sagan speaking so calmly and logically, then Bull Bromfield leaping in with all the tact of a sledgehammer. Not threatening or anything, you know, but making the most awful insinuations—things about how a woman alone out here was taking all kinds of risks. God, I'm tired out just from listening."

She smiled apologetically and sagged into a chair, jabbing at her golden hair with her fingers nervously. She stopped, looked at Ruff, and turned crimson, remembering.

"I nearly got you killed."

"Yes, you did."

"I really am sorry. Things have been piling up. The last hope I had was for that money. Well, it's no excuse."

"Excuse enough. People get under pressure and they usually blow. Most times in the wrong direction. It just has to come out somewhere." Ruff smiled. "Mind if I sit?"

"No." She waved a fluttering hand at the chair across the table from her. He looked around, noticing the wildflowers in the homemade vase on the plank mantel, the braided rag rug, the neatly made bed in the corner.

"Home," she said with a small shrug.

"Don't apologize for it. People seem the happiest, the most comfortable in places like this."

"People who have . . ." Her voice broke off. Ruff saw her eyes go to the high-backed rocker in the corner. Her father's chair, he guessed.

"Well." She smiled and turned a quarter away from him. "You haven't told me what brought you by here."

"Truth is I was looking for the Busby-Blakely mine, and I seem to have missed it."

"It's not easy to find. I'll take you over if you like. But what on earth makes you want to see it? You're not thinking of taking up mining?"

"No." He smiled. "I've seen it done and turned my hand to it a time or two, but that's not only hard work, it's dangerous."

"Your job isn't?"

He smiled again. "It's not the same. I couldn't say why, but it's not. No, the reason I wanted to see the mine was to see where Blakely died. I thought there might be something left to indicate what happened."

"Why, Harlan Busby did it, didn't he?"

"I don't think so. Other people don't either." He told her about the letter, Fist, and Grant Danziger's conviction that the killer had to be a bigger man than Busby.

"I see." She tugged thoughtfully at her lower lip. "But how are you involved in this? Do you know Busby?"

"No. It just happened. I met the man and I can't believe he did it."

"Well," Amy said, "I'll take you over there, but I don't see what you could hope to find."

"I'm not keeping you from your own work?"

"What work? I can't do anything on the claim by myself. Or, I mean to say I can't possibly bring a thousand dollars up out of there by the fifth of July—and that's the deadline."

"A week to find the money, then? Or what happens?"

"I either sell to Bull Bromfield and make a few dollars out of this, or turn it all over to the bank for the note my father took out. Only now"—she sighed—"I don't think Bull Bromfield is going to buy. He was fed up with me, I'm afraid. He'll get it in the end, of course; only I won't see a red cent."

There wasn't much to say to that. Justice didn't have a thousand dollars to give her, knew no one who did. Perhaps with time she could have gotten another buyer interested, but that would mean bringing someone across the plains and no one was traveling that stretch of country just now.

"You've asked for an extension?"

"Of course." She smiled as if that were a joke. "Jack Sagan knows when he's onto a good thing. He smells gold here and plenty of it."

"Your father hit it big?"

"Yes. At least he thought it would be big. That's why he went ahead and borrowed on the place. But the note was sort of complicated: Pa had six months to repay; a survivor—me—became responsible for the whole amount immediately."

"But your father died."

"Yes."

"Amy . . ." Justice hesitated. "Was it an accident?"

"Of course! He fell from his horse. I was so angry I destroyed it myself. No one knows what happened. Perhaps the horse smelled a cougar—there are some prowling around here. But it broke into a run and Father was thrown against a rock beside the trail."

"And his skull was crushed," Justice said with gentle persistence. She didn't want to talk about it, that was obvious, but Justice thought it was necessary.

"Yes."

"In front."

"Really, Mister Justice . . ." She looked ill, remembering. "Yes! If you must know."

Ruff nodded. It probably didn't mean anything. Ruff had the feeling he was reaching for something that wasn't there. Only it was odd, damned odd. Samuel Settle's death had been caused by a wound exactly like Blakely's.

"You have time to ride out to the Busby-Blakely?" he asked, rising abruptly, startling Amy from her unhappy reveries.

"Yes. Yes, I'll get my hat and gloves." She did so, Ruff watching her with those intent blue eyes. She caught his gaze on her and cocked her head to one side questioningly. "See something?"

"Just a pretty girl," he answered.

She laughed out loud. "I don't get told that much."

"Then you're living alone too much. Any man would tell you that, given time."

"You're a strange one, Mister Justice."

"Why? Because I notice pretty women?"

"No. I can't explain it. I don't know if you're teasing me, laughing at me, or laughing at yourself. Maybe at the world."

"I'm not teasing you about being pretty," he answered, and she flushed, pulling on her riding gloves hurriedly.

"Come on, let's have a look at that mine."

Danziger's six miles had stretched into twelve before they came up on the Busby-Blakely mine. On the way Amy had shown Ruff where her father's accident had occurred. The trail was sharply downslanted through a stand of pine trees. Branches overhung the trail and the trail itself was narrow and winding. There was, as far as Ruff could see, only one spot on that trail where the accident could have happened, one spot where the boulders beside it bulged into the roadway itself.

That alone bothered him. He got down and poked around the stand of boulders while Amy stood, arms folded, looking into the distances, toward the bald mountain.

"Anything?" she asked when he returned.

"Not a thing."

"What is it exactly that you wanted to find? It was an accident. I've accepted it. Everyone has."

"Yes." Everyone except Ruff Justice, who was beginning to get a bad feeling about things in general. Bear Fork was gold country, and where there was gold, there was avarice and frequently bloodshed.

Sometimes it was even accidental.

"I've been wondering about the Morgan gang," Ruff said, swinging aboard the roan. "You know, Sheriff Marks had a chance to pull in Art Morgan and he didn't do it."

"Marks!" she snorted. "It's not likely he'd try anything against the Morgans. I was surprised he stopped the fight in the street." She colored again, recalling who it was that had caused that. "The Morgans," she went on, collecting herself, "have done a lot of things. Murder among them, I suppose. But Bear Fork was home ground. They had the sense not to pull anything around here. Nothing, that is, except for the saloon brawls and general hell-raising. You know how the local law is in areas like this. No one wanted to pursue the Morgans across the plains—just too much trouble. It must have been close to election time in Bismarck, or else Shearer was the exception.

"They roamed about doing pretty much what they wanted; then, when they had their saddlebags full, they headed home. To Bear Fork. They're supposed to have a hideout up on that bald mountain. I guess they do." She slapped the long runner, which was trying to reach back and bite her leg.

Ruff realized now why she had needed the horse. She had killed her father's horse out of rage and grief. It was difficult now to think of Amy doing such a thing, but Justice remembered the ferocity in her green eyes the day he had ridden into Bear Fork. She was capable of doing it, all right. And capable of killing a man if she had to.

"Here we are. It's a mile or so up this trail. That's funny," she said. "Wagon tracks, and new ones."

That they were. The tracks of heavy wagons with wide wheels running up the road through the timber toward the Busby-Blakely mine.

"Why, someone's working the mine," Amy said in puzzlement.

"No one should be." Not with Blakely dead and Busby in jail for his murder. Ruff frowned and started up the trail, Amy beside him. They didn't get far.

The man with the shotgun stepped out of the trees and planted himself in the middle of the road.

"That's far enough. You can just turn around and ride back out."

"We can, can we?" Amy flared up. "And just who are you to tell us that?"

"I'm the man with the scattergun, lady," he said, drawing back the double hammers of his weapon. "That enough authority?"

"It is for me," Ruff said mildly. "Come on, Amy."

"Why should we go?" She was still hot. "We don't even know who this man is. Who's up at the mine? They have no business there."

"You a lawyer, are you?" the guard asked. He turned

his head and spat. "Just go on along now. I never shot no woman, and I don't intend to. Neither," he added, "are you going to come through here. I've got my orders and I mean to earn my pay."

Ruff had to take Amy's bridle and turn her horse. She was still fuming when they reached the main road again. "Why did you let him push you around? They've got no business up there. Who were they?"

"The same people," Ruff guessed, "who will be at your claim the day the bank forecloses."

They rode a mile down the trail and pulled off into the trees. The sun was warm, the sky clear. The grass was long and sweet. Spring had come late to Dakota—it was nearly the Fourth of July—but it had come gloriously. The birds sang in the tall timber. Gentian and bluebells spotted the grass in the meadows with patches of color.

Ruff loosened the cinches on both horses and sat down cross-legged on the grass beside Amy, who was furiously pulling up stalks of grama, hurling them aside.

"It's getting so that you can't go anywhere," she complained to the miles of wilderness before her. She glanced at Ruff then, abashed, and smiled. "There goes that temper of mine again. But just who were they, Ruff?"

"Miners. That's all. As to who sent them out—well, it has to be either Sagan or Bromfield, doesn't it? Likely both of them."

"Well, they didn't waste any time, did they?"

"No. They don't waste time when gold is at stake. It's got to be illegal, as you say, but then, how would anyone stop it? By the time a circuit judge came in, Busby would be hanged, Blakely dead, and probably it would be found that the bank had claimed the mine for taxes."

"But what about Mrs. Busby? Harlan has a wife, you know."

"Yes, I know." And Justice hadn't yet gotten around to seeing her, to make sure the "old lady" was all right as he promised Busby. "Can we go by later?"

"Yes, of course. I've met Emily Busby only once, but that's the least we can do. And she should know that someone is on her husband's claim."

"Yes. If she doesn't already know."

"What do you mean?"

"She would need money now. Maybe she just happened to get a helpful offer from Mister Sagan at the bank." Ruff shrugged. "We'll drop around and see."

"Yes."

She was looking at him still, but Ruff realized suddenly that she wasn't thinking of Mrs. Busby or of the mine or of the Morgan gang. Nor was he.

The grass was sweet-smelling, cabbage moths fluttered past just out of reach. The breeze carried the scent of pine and cedar to them across the meadow, and Ruff lifted a hand, placed it on her shoulder, and drew Amy to him.

Her breath quickened and he felt her lips resist, part, soften, and briefly tense again. He let her go and she sat up, watching him with amazement, her green eyes wide and alert.

"Mister Justice," she said, and Ruff drew her to him again, his arms going around her as he rolled onto his back and lay against the prickly grass.

Amy was against him, hesitant but wanting. Her lips met his, touched the point of his chin, brushed across his forehead, and she smiled as Ruff's hands slid down her back to her waist, then up the flare of her firm hips.

She sighed and sagged against him, the tenseness going out of her, and Ruff kissed her throat, feeling the pulse there. Her hand brushed back his dark hair and she looked deeply into his eyes before her lips parted again, revealing even white teeth. She leaned forward, kissing him deeply this time, her tongue darting between his lips, searching his mouth as Ruff's hands clenched her buttocks and drew her pelvis close against him.

She lay back, her fingers toying with the fringes of his buckskin shirt, and she closed her eyes as Ruff slowly began to unbutton the cotton shirt she wore, his lips grazing her breasts, following his deft fingers down to her navel, flitting across her smooth belly.

He helped her from her shirt and lay propped up on one elbow for a time, his hand running across her ripe, round breasts, teasing the pink buds of her nipples. Amy, behind closed eyelids, focused on the warmth of the day, the knowing hands, the rising sensation in her breasts, the flush of her face, the growing warmth between her legs.

When he lay against her again, he had removed his shirt. His hard chest pressed against her, flattening her breasts. His kisses danced across her jawline and down her throat, across breasts and belly, dropping lower, and she felt his fingers at her trouser buttons.

She shifted to help him remove them. She felt her trousers slip down, felt him slide her boots from her feet, and then she was naked against the grass, naked as the warm sun beamed down and the birds sang distantly, the breeze rippling through the trees.

He was naked now, too, rolling to her, his muscular thighs pressed against her until inexorably her knees parted and Ruff Justice slid between them, his lips still tasting throat and breasts, ear and eyelid, moving ceaselessly as his hands ran across the silk of her inner thighs. Amy gave a slight shudder, feeling the slow urging of her body, the liquid warmth of it, the needful awakening of her inner muscles.

Her hands darted between her legs and she found him there, ready and warm, solid. She positioned him, her head lolling, her mouth open, her breathing ragged, and with tiny motions of her hips she urged him on.

Slowly he entered her and she felt herself blossoming. Her hands reached behind him and clenched the hard-muscled buttocks of Ruff Justice.

Amy's legs lifted and she locked them behind Ruff, her heart racing frantically now as he slowly and methodically drove against her, pinning her to the grass, flooding her with sensation.

She wanted to hurry him, to shriek at him to do it quicker, to split her open. She bit now at a knuckle, her eyes tightly closed in concentration as his pelvis met hers time and again, and the world seemed to spin around crazily, the ground beneath her to lift up until she burst in sensual flowering, her breathing rapid, labored, her fingers clutching at his back and shoulders, his buttocks, drawing him in until in exhaustion she lay back, a single tear escaping her eye to run down across her flushed cheek.

It was hours, days, eternities, before she stirred again, before she wanted to move, to let him go; but finally, her body seemingly nerveless, incapable of any motion, her legs slackened their grip, her heart slowed its steady hammering, and she realized that he was simply lying there, looking down at her with that slight smile playing about his lips, a warm and yet enigmatic smile.

"Was I asleep?" She yawned.

"Only for a minute. We'd better get going, don't you think?"

"I suppose." She stretched her arms and then wrapped them around Justice again. "If you say so."

"Yes." He got up and offered her a hand up. Then he held her for a minute, stroking her back, his nostrils filled with the ripe scent of her sun-warmed golden hair. "Let's go, then," he said, not without reluctance, and she nodded, pulling away before either of them could change his mind.

The day grew warmer yet, although the sun had nearly reached the bald mountain on its downward arc. For the first time Justice became aware that it was nearly July. There was no breeze now on the dusty downslanting trail toward the Busby house, and the scent of the pines was nearly oppressive.

"Right there," Amy said, and Ruff glanced at the stone cabin set back among the trees. It wasn't a cheerful-looking place. No flowers had been planted. Weeds grew up beside the house. No smoke rose from the chimney. A pair of molting hens scratched patiently at the bare yard before the house.

Ruff got down to open the gate and the rifle boomed out. A section of fence only a foot from his hand was blown away, spattering him with bark.

"You, get!" the voice from the cabin shouted. "You get out of here before I blow your head off, Ruffin Justice!"

7

Justice didn't argue with the rifle. He was aboard the roan and into the timber, leading the long runner and Amy. She appeared pale, her mood suddenly, inexplicably shattered by the gunfire.

"That was Emily Busby's voice," Amy hissed into his ear.

"Yes. I thought it was." Ruff stood beside his horse, looking through the trees at the stone cabin.

"She must have gone mad."

"Maybe. Maybe the whole country has. Everyplace I go someone seems to be trying to kill me."

"How could she have known your name?" Amy started to swing up on the chestnut. "I'm going to go down there and tell her everything's all right. She won't shoot at me if I'm alone."

"Maybe not." Ruff shook his head. "I don't like you taking that chance. She sounded wound up, really wound up. She's liable to shoot anything that moves, Amy."

"I can't believe it."

"There are other ways of doing it. We can get around to the back of the house through the trees. If she thinks she drove us off, she won't be expecting it."

"This whole thing doesn't make any sense to me," Amy said in exasperation.

"No? It seems to me it's starting to make a lot of sense, Amy. Think about it."

She just shook her head, not knowing what he was getting at. Together they returned to the gate, turned their horses away and back up the trail, their spines crawling—who knew what the mind behind those gunsights was thinking? They rode for a quarter of a mile, then turned back into the trees, circling wide toward the stone cabin where Harlan Busby's temporarily unbalanced wife would be waiting, rifle in hand . . . and she could shoot that thing, Ruff reminded himself. That hadn't been any chance shot she had stung him with.

When they could see the roof of the house through the trees, Ruff swung down, handing the reins to the roan up to Amy. She started to voice some objection, but Ruff, placing a cautioning finger to his lips, silenced her.

Leaving her in the trees, he slipped toward the house, working down a rock-littered gulley that brought him out of the trees behind a leaning, weathered shack. He could see the back door of the cabin from there, see the wash hung on a line.

There was no window in the back, and that made things easier. Ruff wasn't taking this lightly, however. That frightened woman was as dangerous as any Sioux just now. She had a gun and had shown both the ability and the inclination to use it.

In a crouch he darted across the yard, his own pistol holstered. He was suddenly against the house, his back pressed against the rough stone of the wall. Five feet away was the door, the latch string drawn in. He hoped it wasn't as solid as it looked.

It would have to be quick. Mrs. Busby could be just behind the door waiting. He would have to take that chance. Stepping out, Ruff shouldered the door and it popped free of its wooden hinges to collapse against the kitchen floor with a crash.

Justice had never stopped moving, and as the stout woman in frock and apron came through the inner door, eyes wide, rifle raised, Justice merely stepped to her and wrenched it from her hands.

She looked up into his eyes, opened her mouth as if to scream, and them simply folded up and sagged to the floor before Ruff could catch her.

"What happened?" Amy, not minding very well, had come after Justice and now she rushed into the kitchen.

"Just fainted. I thought I told you to stay in the timber."

"Bossy aren't you?" Amy asked. She was crouched down over Mrs. Busby. "Can you find some water?"

"You might have gotten yourself hurt," Justice said. He found the pewter pitcher on the table, a cup beside it, and brought it to Amy, who was crouched down on the floor, Mrs. Busby's head propped up on her knee.

"Can we move her into the other room?"

"I think so," Ruff said. Already she was showing signs of coming around. Ruff hooked Emily Busby under the arms and Amy took the woman's feet. They carried her into the cabin's other room and placed her on the settee, feet propped up. In another minute she was alert enough to be frightened all over again.

"Don't kill me," she said pathetically.

"No one's going to touch a hair on your head," Ruff said.

"Emily? It's me, Amy Settle. You remember me." Amy knelt down beside the woman and placed a damp cloth on her forehead. Her eyes searched Amy's face and seemed to quiet a little.

"What's happening here?" Amy wanted to know. "Who's got you so frightened?"

"They said someone would be coming around . . . someone who wanted the mine and didn't care how he got it."

"Who said that?"

"They said he was a tall man in buckskins . . . that his name was Ruff Justice."

"Who said it, Emily?" Amy Settle repeated quietly. She patted the old woman's hand, reassuring her as Ruff crouched down in the far corner, watching and listening.

"I'm not supposed to say—" Her eyes went to Ruff, then quickly veered away.

"All right. I think we know anyway. It was Mister Sagan and Bull Bromfield, wasn't it?"

The old woman's eyes gave her away, but she made no answer.

"I don't know what to do. Everyone wants the claim. Yet at the same time they all tell me it's worthless." She gripped Amy's hand more tightly. "Why do they all want it if it's worthless? I just don't know what to do. I can't work the mine, and Harlan . . . Harlan won't be coming back, will he?" Her eyes suddenly were flooded with tears and she began sobbing, throwing her forearm across her face to hide her grief.

Ruff spoke for the first time. "Your husband will be coming back, Mrs. Busby. I'll see to it."

"Back!" She laughed hysterically. "Yes, when I bury him out back under that oak tree."

"No. He'll be back alive. I promise you."

Emily Busby just stared at him. Her head rolled toward the tall man, her tear-glossed eyes wide, wanting to believe, not quite managing it.

"How can . . . ?"

"I promise you. Now don't worry about it. And don't worry about the mine. You'll know what to do when the time comes. Meanwhile just don't sell it."

Amy was furious when Ruff went with her to the kitchen to start hot water for tea.

"How could you make her a promise like that! Just how are you going to get Harlan Busby out of jail before they hang him?"

"I will." He leaned against the wall, arms folded. "Maybe you're right, maybe I shouldn't have promised her that, but I meant it. For the time being he's in the best place possible. The only place, maybe, where he can stay alive for a while."

"Are you trying to make a joke?" Amy was searching for a match to start the stove fire and Ruff handed her one, thumbing it to light it. "He's under sentence of death and you say he's lucky to be in jail waiting to die."

"Yes. I'll tell you what I think, Amy. I couldn't prove it in a court, or anywhere else, but I think I know what's been happening around here.

"Sagan and Bromfield want the three mines down south here. They seem to want them very badly. Maybe they've about played out the Amalgamated veins, I don't know. Things began happening a few months back. First off, Blakely was killed and they arrested Harlan Busby for the murder. That got both of them out of the way.

"Next, your father was killed—it was supposed to be an accident, but I doubt it very much. According to what I've heard, his injury was very similar to that which killed Blakely. And if we accept the fact that Busby didn't kill his partner—and I do—then we've got to think that the same person murdered your father."

"Murdered!"

"Yes. It was a clever job, as Blakely's death was cleverly handled, but I think it was murder. That took care of two of the mines and their owners, leaving them only two frightened and upset women to deal with. You they had in a barrel. That note your father took out played right into their hands. Maybe Sagan himself suggested it, I don't know. After the fifth of July you won't count anymore."

Amy placed the tea kettle on to boil and stood watching Ruff, her mind slowly turning over everything he had said. "What about Grant Danziger? He's got a claim down here."

"Yes, but Danziger was out when the assayers' report came back so decidedly negative. Now he's in again, unfortunately. He's got a rich copper strike up there, and by now Sagan probably knows it."

"Then he'll have to be killed. Oh, Ruff! Why did you tell Emily not to sell out? If she won't give way, they'll kill her too, won't they?"

Justice didn't answer. He looked at Amy with cold blue eyes. "Your kettle's boiling."

While she steeped the tea, he went on, "What has bothered me is the fact that when the mail rider was killed, the mail stolen, only three letters were saved. The rest were burned, but not these three—the three that had some bearing on Bear Fork troubles: your uncle's note to you, the tip that Fist might know who really killed Blakely, the assayers' report to Grant Danziger."

"The Morgan gang is based not far from here. You think they meant to do something with that information?"

"I think they meant to turn the letters over to Bull Bromfield or Sagan—it doesn't matter which, it's obvious they're working together."

"I don't know." Amy poked nervously at her golden hair. "It all seems to make sense, yet I can't believe Sagan is so cold-blooded."

"There's a lot at stake. If those claims up north are running out of high-grade ore, then Sagan is finished. Finished because without the mines there is no Bear

Fork, no Bear Fork bank. If this town is like most, Sagan's got money invested in those buildings, loans to the citizens, probably a considerable amount of capital in Bromfield's mines. Yes, he would be cold-blooded when it came to being wiped out or removing a few insignificant prospectors. Bromfield—well, you don't have to see much of him to know that it wouldn't bother his conscience a bit."

"I don't like this, Ruff. It scares me." She was pouring Emily Busby's tea, her eyes going to the inner door. "She'll have to go into town."

"You too. You can both stay at the hotel."

"Why should I be run off?" Amy asked, her temper mounting again.

"Someone," Ruff said gently, moving nearer, kissing her flushed cheek, "should watch Mrs. Busby, don't you think?"

"I suppose so." Amy sighed. "All right. What about this Fist?"

"I don't know what about him. No one seems to know where he is, and I have the feeling no one's going to find him unless he wants to be found."

"But if you don't find him, Harlan Busby is going to hang."

"Yes." Ruff smiled, but there wasn't a lot of humor in it. "Let's give the woman her tea while it's warm."

The town of Bear Fork was heating up for the Fourth of July celebration. Red, white, and blue bunting was hanging from several buildings, a banner was hung across the street. Ruff studied it all gloomily. He didn't care much for most holidays, which seemed to be nothing more than an excuse for people to get drunk and raise hell. Generally someone got hurt.

The hotel was surprisingly neat. The lobby was carpeted, although the rough plank walls marked the place as a frontier establishment. The clerk was dressed in suit and tie. There were paintings on the walls, a genuine mahogany banister on the staircase leading up to the second floor. Maybe the hotel owner had had dreams of Bear Fork turning into another Denver, a wild town where money meant nothing, where they had more gold and silver than they knew what to do with, where people had castles from Europe shipped stone by stone to them, where bathtubs in the wealthier homes were made of gold, where the hotels were flooded with millionaires begging for something to spend their money on.

It hadn't happened. There was a forced gaiety in the room clerk's manner. The hotel reminded Ruff of an old maid sitting and waiting endlessly for suitors who would never come.

Amy and Emily Busby took adjoining rooms on the second floor, near the end of the corridor. Ruff asked for, and with some difficulty got, the spare keys to the rooms, which he pocketed.

There was a view of the hills from Mrs. Busby's room, but it wasn't real attractive. There the smoke rose. The skies were gray with it. Rain had stripped the naked slopes of soil. He saw her standing looking out the window and wondered where her thoughts were, wondered if those bleak and denuded hills reflected her own gloom.

"I'll want to see Harlan right away. As soon as I've washed up. Do you think that will be all right, Amy? You don't think he'll mind?"

"He'll be pleased," Amy said, casting a pathetic glance at Ruff Justice.

Ruff's thoughts were already elsewhere. If he wanted to place his head on the chopping block for Sagan and Bromfield, he couldn't do it in a better way than he had planned. He had to try to find Fist, had to at least make the attempt. That meant riding toward the bald mountain.

That put him alone in unknown country—in the country where what was left of the Morgan gang had its stronghold. Art Morgan wouldn't have forgotten—he owed Ruff now. As to Jake, he was reputed to be worse than his brother, the old bull of the herd.

The Morgans were, had to be, tied in with Sagan and Bromfield. There was no other explanation for saving those three letters from the fire.

Sheriff Marks? Well, maybe so and maybe not, but there was no point in going to him with his speculations. The sheriff believed in letting sleeping dogs lie. He sure as hell wasn't going to help Ruff Justice on the strength of what he had.

"You'll stay here, won't you, Amy?" He had caught up with her next to the window that faced the west, where the lowering sun painted the hills with shifting shadows, glinted blue and golden on the glass panes. He had her by the shoulders and he felt her body go slack, and he kissed her, holding her tightly for a moment.

"Stay with me," she said breathily.

"I can't or I would."

"When it's over?"

"Or before." Ruff smiled. "But I made the old woman a promise, you know." He only wished he could think of something to do for Amy. Where in hell could a man out here come by a thousand dollars in a few days? Nowhere was the answer; he had only the vague hope that when the Sagan-Bromfield house fell down, Amy would somehow wriggle free. He kissed her again, paused a moment to look at the rigid back of Emily Busby before the window in the other room. "Lock these doors and keep them locked," he reminded her. Then he spun on his heel and was out the door and down the stairs.

Ruff went out into the street, noticing the carpenters building a grandstand for the Fourth of July festivities. He turned toward the general store and went in, a little bell on the door tinkling to bring a small, bald-headed, shirt-sleeved man from the back room.

"Something?" he asked with the brevity of one who doesn't speak much of the language. He was a Swede, or perhaps a Norwegian, Ruff guessed.

"A hat, first off," Justice told him. He had done without one long enough. "Then I'll need some food. A few things for the trail."

"Leaving us, Mister Justice?"

Ruff hadn't heard the bell tinkle. Maybe Hawkes had been there all along. He was lounging near the cracker barrel, reading a month-old Fargo newspaper, the *Daily Commercial*.

"Yes. There's nothing for me to do around here."

"We got the Fourth coming up." He winked at the storekeeper, who was balancing a dozen hats of different styles and colors as he walked toward the counter. "Sack races, shooting contest, horse race. The hotel's put together a brass band."

"Enjoy it," Ruff said. "Me, I'm leaving."

Hawkes tried not to show it, but he was satisfied with that answer. He waved good-bye to the storekeeper and went out, undoubtedly to report to Sheriff Marks, who would report to Sagan that Ruff was leaving.

"What size is the white one?" Justice asked.

Ten minutes later he was at the stable taking the roan away from its comfort, exchanging scornful glances with the long runner, which snorted and stamped a hoof.

"Crusty old bastard, ain't it?" the stableboy grumbled.

"Watch yourself—he bites."

"Don't I know it!"

In another half-hour Ruff was saddled, provisioned,

and mounted, riding out of Bear Fork and toward the great bald mountain ahead of him. A fool riding a fool's trail, he told himself. If Fist was there, he had only a slim chance of finding him. The odds were much better indeed that he would find the Morgans and be left to dry on the slopes.

Ruff Justice tugged town the brim of his new white hat and rode on, winding through the piny hills toward the peak ahead of him, whistling as he rode, sometimes breaking off to curse himself for the fool that he was.

8

Justice stayed away from the traveled roads and moved slowly across country, through the warm, dry, piney hills. Jays squawked in the trees and one followed him for a way, hopping from bough to bough, accusing the interloper.

Now and then the trees fell away and he got a clear view of the bald mountain standing stolid and aloof beneath a pale sky. His task seemed futile the nearer he got. How in hell was he going to find Fist? How could he live with himself if he didn't make the attempt? There was a man sitting in the Bear Fork jail who was counting his life in hours now, and he hadn't many hours left.

Ruff camped that evening on a twisted, gully-scoured hill that overlooked the long valley below. From there he could see all the way back to Bear Fork, see the faint milky glow of its lights.

There was another light against the dark land, this farther ahead, nearer to the mountain. A campfire dull and wavering, like a winking red eye in the distance.

It could have been anyone, but Justice had the idea it wasn't Fist. No Indian would build a fire that large, that exposed. Not a lone Indian traveling scared.

Was he scared? It seemed likely. If not scared, then

cautious. He had witnessed some white man's crime and had the sense to get out.

Not Fist. The Morgans? That was more likely. They had no fear of the law, not in this area.

It could also have been any rover, prospector, hunter, homesteader. It was too far for Ruff to investigate on this night anyway, so he marked its position relative to the surrounding landforms and shifted his attention to the vast wilderness surrounding him. The hour was late, and after boiling coffee, he leaned back against a pine and sat sipping it, watching the velvet-shadowed hills, the long plains beyond, which showed only as a deep black sea. He sat and watched the land go dark, watched the sullen, pale, pock-faced moon rise gently in the east, and he thought of the little golden-haired girl he had left back in Bear Fork, of the compact strength of her lithe young body . . . Those thoughts were no good on a night like this.

He yawned, rose, and checked that the roan was picketed properly and could reach graze, then he spread out his bedroll and sank into a dreamless, heavy sleep.

With the dawn he was riding again, higher into the hills, toward the bald mountain, which seemed to grow higher, starker as he approached it. Now he rode along steeply pitched slopes where ghostly stands of dead timber stood, where the roan had difficulty picking its way across the tangle of deadfalls, rock slides, suddenly appearing crevices that forced Ruff to backtrack a dozen times in a mile.

His attention was on the trail ahead of him, but his blue eyes constantly shifted up and down the slopes as well, searching for anything that didn't belong, a flash of color, sunlight on metal, the geometric shape of a man-made structure.

But he saw nothing for mile after mile but the jumble of wilderness-born monuments: skeletons of dead trees; shelves and crags of white limestone and black basalt, rivers of broken shale littering the hillside, the wind howling down the long slopes were the only presences.

The land uptilted and grew more broken yet. Ruff was perspiring as he lifted his eyes to the bald peak above him, to the barren white slopes where nothing grew. It was like looking above the timberline in the Rockies, seeing the cold sterility of naked rock—only, here there was no snow. Even at this altitude it was hot and dry, the breeze increasing his discomfort, not alleviating it.

He had to get down now and lead the roan. He didn't dwell on the madness of this effort: seeking a man who didn't want to be found in this devil's playground, a man who knew the wild ways better than he did, who could hide beneath a stone, who could lay motionless for hours in the torpid heat, who would be a shadow flitting across the rocky mountain when he moved.

He trudged on, leading the roan, which had become balky. It was not bred for this. It was a horse meant for cutting out cattle on the flat Texas plains, quick and agile. But it was gutty and strong, young and capable.

Just then Ruff wasn't sure he shared any of those qualities. He was sweating profusely, his feet were leaden, the muscles in his thighs knotted as he climbed laboriously up the shattered slopes, going to his knees time after time.

And then there was a trail, ancient and worn, beginning suddenly, winding up the mountain, appearing no wider than an eyebrow.

The trail was old, very old—formed, before history had begun, by the feet of an ancient people, one that had roamed this land before the Sioux, before the Cheyenne, before memory.

It wasn't the first time Justice had seen such a trail. Now and then, especially in the Southwest, one stumbled across them, and following them to their head came to a crumbled cliff dwelling, a geometric patch of cleared earth, sometimes with great symbols carved into it: descriptions, prayers, indications of where they had gone and why. Who knew? The language was gone and the people had vanished with the wind.

He was higher yet. The trail broadened enough so that Justice was once more able to mount the roan. The trees had gone now, fallen away. There was no brush, not so much as a blade of grass. Nothing but the white stone, the vast dome of the mountain.

Justice came around the shoulder of the hill slope, dipped down into the ravine and up the other side. The rifle cracked and Ruff felt the searing pain in his chest as he was lifted from the saddle and hurled to the ground, the roan dancing away in panic, the echoes rolling down the slope. Somewhere above harsh laughter sounded, and Justice, staggering to his feet, clawed at his empty holster, dragging himself back to the trail. He fell again and lay there stunned by pain.

He could see his Colt a few yards down the trail and he got to his feet, breaking into a stumbling run, gripping his chest where the hot blood welled up, staining his buckskin shirt.

Before he could reach his pistol, a second and third shot sounded, whining off the rock face beside him, and turning, Justice saw the three men on horseback riding down on him from above.

He saw and recognized Art Morgan in that split second before he reached his decision. He had to go over, down off the cliff into the chasm at his feet. There was no way up, no other way to avoid their guns.

Justice leaped, hearing the staccato reports of their guns. His hair streamed out behind him, his eyes were wide, seeing the great distances, gray-white and hazy, and the terrible broken columns of stone below him.

He had time to draw his legs up under him so that they wouldn't be broken, and then he hit solid rock, hit it hard, the breath being driven from his body by the impact, the force of upward-driving knees.

He hit, skidded, jolted head and shoulder against stone, rolled, and came to a stop against a jagged, weathered outcropping, still hearing the thunder of the guns above him, hearing Art Morgan scream over and over, "Find him! Kill the bastard!"

Then Justice heard no more. Crumpled against the outcropping, the world spinning madly past him, his chest shot full of pain, he passed out, knowing that they would find him now. They would kill him, and just then it didn't seem that it would matter very much. The darkness yawned and swallowed him.

When you went down below, there were thousands of them, all playing tom-toms, banging them and screaming as they danced around the black flames. They had women with arrows piercing their breasts. Toothless things with fire in their mouths. They could see right through you and they knew what you were. If you moved, they jabbed you with fiery lances. One of them had a sack full of faces and they made you look in it, an iron-hard hand gripping the back of your neck, shoving your head into the stink of it, into the laughter that rose from the faces.

When they tired of that, they hung you to a tree and set fire to it, watching the flames lick your feet and legs. They sat in quiet circles, arms looped around their knees, watching as the flames mounted higher, the pain so intense that you had to scream out, shattering them all to fragments of black glass . . .

Ruff came awake, his heart pounding, and he could see nothing at all. It was still black. He thought he had gone blind until he noticed the hazy glow of the coming moon against the night sky.

He thought that he had died until the pain came

surging back, like the fiery agony of his nightmare, but worse. He felt his throat constrict, felt the muscles bunch to loose a scream, and he clamped his teeth together until they hurt. If he cried out, they'd come and finish the job.

"So, you are awake."

Ruff's head turned sharply; his hand dipped to his belt sheath, searching for the familiar grip of the bowie knife, but it was gone and the man crouching over him chuckled.

"Yes, I found it. And I took the one in your boot too."

"Fist."

"Yes." The old Indian cocked his head. "Be quiet, though, or they will return. They could not find you, but Fist found you."

"How did you . . . ?"

"Quiet," he said more forcefully. "You must be still. Let me see what has happened."

Ruff felt his shirt being cut open by a razor-sharp knife, his own skinning knife, he thought. He felt the gentle hands doing something to the gunshot wound that filled him with a savage pain he couldn't suppress, and then he felt nothing again. He sank into the deep and silent void where there was no knowledge, no awareness, and no pain.

It was still dark when his eyes fluttered open again. He had been moved; that he realized immediately. The rocks no longer bit at his flesh, and looking up, he couldn't see the sky. No moon, no stars, just a smoky outline of something that must have been the roof to a lean-to.

Outside, the wind creaked in the pines. He heard footsteps approaching, reached automatically for a weapon before realizing he had none, and tensed himself for a last struggle.

The silhouette appeared in the doorway. Tall, lean,

bent, and the old Indian came forward, carrying something. A bowl or basket.

"Are you awake?" he asked.

"Yes. Did I dream it, or are you Fist?"

"I am Fist. Do I know you, Hunter?"

"No. But I've been looking for you . . ." Ruff's voice broke off as the Indian tore a bandage from his wound and began applying a poultice of some kind. It smelled faintly of sage. The hands were gentle, but the pain stabbed through him. He felt the sweat raining off his body. The old Indian chanted under his breath as he worked in the darkness.

"They will not find you here," Fist said. "They have not found me."

"The Morgans?"

"If that is their name. Men with beards. Hold still now. You talk too much."

Ruff went out again then and he was aware of nothing until a demanding hunger began tightening his stomach and he opened encrusted eyes to see that the sun was shining. He lay watching it for a minute dreamily until reality came home with a rush. He was lying on his back high up on a mountain, hunted by outlaws. He had left a girl and a woman down below waiting for his help, left a man in prison who would be hung if Justice didn't return with some evidence to save him.

He sat up, felt pain gnaw at his chest, felt his head swim. Looking down, he saw that his chest was bandaged up tightly, that his shirt was gone, the knees torn out of his buckskin pants. His bowie and skinning knives lay beside him now and he picked them up, tucking them away in their sheaths.

Then he got unsteadily to his feet, holding on to the lean-to's upright until the world stopped spinning, then he hobbled out into the piercingly bright light of morning.

The old Mandan sat before a low fire, eating from a bowl with his fingers. He was facing away from Ruff, looking out across the long valleys, the endless hills, but he greeted Ruff.

"Good morning, Hunter. Are you well enough to eat?"

"I'm well enough, Fist. I'd better eat standing, though. If I get down, I don't think I'll make it up again."

Fist filled a bowl and brought it to Justice, who was leaning precariously against a pine tree. In the moment he had had to look around him Justice had seen that they were camping on a ledge overhanging a valley. The drop to it seemed very sheer. It was all of three thousand feet down. Behind them the mountain rose in tiers. Justice could see no way up out of there either.

All around them the bald mountain, barren and inhospitable, rose. Only here was there a pocket of green, a few trees, a little rill winking in the sunlight as it ran across the ledge and careened off into space, misting into the air as it fell.

Fist handed Ruff his bowl and they stood looking at each other for a moment, measuring.

"You are strong, you will heal," Fist said finally. "Many old battle wounds on you, Hunter. You are a warrior?"

"Army scout."

"White scout?" Fist smiled distantly. "Yes," he said without intonation.

"How did you find me, Fist?"

"The shots. The men with beards were pursuing me. They would never catch Fist, but they do not know this. I was going up the mountain to the old stronghold, you see." He held a sharply angled hand in front of Ruff's face. "Very steep. No horse can climb so steep as a man, so I was away. Then they began shooting and I pressed myself flat. But the bullets did not come. They were shooting away from me. I saw them hit you. I saw you fall.

"The men with the beards saw it too, but they have white eyes—I am sorry, Hunter, but it is so—they have white eyes and so they did not see the rock where you fell. They believed you had gone far below to the bottom of the canyon. And so they believed you dead."

Ruff had been eating greedily all through this speech, which Fist delivered with many gestures. The food was made of cornmeal and meat. Justice had no idea what you would call it, but it was warm, tasty, and filling. He scraped at the bottom of the bowl, and Fist, smiling, took it to refill it.

"Yes," he said, "you will live. The bullet went through, like this." He pulled at his own slack breast and jabbed a finger into it. "Side to side. The muscles are cut, but they will grow together. Much blood was lost, but you are building more blood already. You must simply rest. A week, maybe two, and you will be strong enough to travel again."

"I haven't got a week," Justice said.

"Why is this, Hunter? You have a man to kill?"

"Perhaps. And one to save."

"So?" Fist's eyebrows raised. "I like a good story, Hunter. Have you a story of war and vengeance for me?"

"Yes," Ruff Justice said, "and you're a part of it, Fist."

"I do not understand. It is me you wish to kill, or me you must save?" the old Mandan asked with a smile.

"It is you who can save a man, Fist. Or another man—since you've surely saved my life."

"This is nothing." He shrugged. "To care for a man who has been hurt, to feed him? Would I not want someone to do the same for me? But this other—I do not understand what man I can save, how I could do such a thing."

"Do you know the Busby-Blakely mine?"

"Which one is this? So many holes in the ground, all the same."

"The one where a man was murdered."

Fist's eyes suddenly became wary. The congenial light went out of them and he turned half away. "I do not know."

"You were there."

"If you say so."

"And you saw it."

"If you say so, Hunter."

"Listen to me, Fist. They've arrested that man's partner and they're going to hang him. He didn't commit that murder. I know this and you know it."

"Perhaps I know this. Perhaps I was there."

"You've got to go into Bear Fork and tell the sheriff that."

"No. No, I do not think so. Who will believe me anyway, Hunter? Once I saw the army make a trial with one white man who was very bad, one Indian who was very truthful. The soldiers said, 'An Indian's word is no good. All Indians are liars.' And so they took the Indian and shot him. It was so. It will be so again if I go to Bear Fork."

"It won't happen that way. I'll be with you."

"No. Men will come to kill me then. Men who did the murder. Or they will lock me in the prison to wait for the trial. That I could not stand, Hunter. I think I do not remember what I saw."

He was adamant. No argument Ruff could come up with could change Fist's mind. He was certain that either he would be placed under protective custody, locked in the jailhouse, or he would be killed before he could speak at a trial.

He was probably right.

"Will you tell me, then, Fist? At least tell me what you saw—I can tell the sheriff, though he probably won't believe me, and I know it won't be accepted as evidence in any trial."

Fist rubbed his cheek and looked again to the distances, apparently debating with himself.

"Yes," he said finally. "Yes, I will tell you what I saw that day."

Ruff had finished his second bowl of food and he handed it back to Fist, who dropped it near the fire, which was nearly burned out. Then the old Indian paced from side to side, speaking as if the story were one passed down for a hundred years instead of an incident that had happened before his eyes not many months ago.

"There was a place where white men went to dig up gold from the earth. There were many such, but at this one there was also a Mandan named Fist. Fist was a poor Indian, unjustly banished from his tribe. Fist had to take what he could find to live. He had no wife to make him a blanket when the winter was coming. He had no friends to share home or food.

"Fist, on a certain morning, was near the place where the white men dug, and he looked toward them because voices were raised in argument—but then white men always argue over nothing.

"Fist did not hear what the argument was about. He saw the two men, one very big, with the shoulders of a bear, one not nearly so big."

"Blakely and Busby," Ruff said, but Fist went on as if there had been no interruption.

"Finally the smaller man goes away angrily, into the hole they have dug. The big one laughs first, then gets to his own work. Nothing else happens and so Fist sits back to eat the breakfast he has foraged.

"Not long after, Fist hears the approaching horse

and he rolls onto his belly and wriggles nearer to look down upon the mine again. Another man has arrived, a big man, nearly as big as the miner who works there.

"There is shouting before the newcomer has even gotten from his horse. 'Go away! Get out of here! I told you I did not wish to see you again!' But the other man comes anyway and stands with his fists clenched, speaking quietly."

"What did he look like?" Ruff asked.

Fist looked annoyed at having his recital cut off, but he answered. "Very big. White."

"Yes. Did he have a beard?"

"No. Only nose-whiskers. A moustache, like this." Fist placed a straightened finger beneath his nose.

"Bromfield."

"As you say." Fist shrugged as if it were of no importance. He went on with his story. "The men stood together talking angrily. Then the miner turns away, very angry, disgusted. Fist sees the new man with the moustache go back to his horse, but he does not leave. He takes a club from his saddle and walks to where the miner still works, now bent over, facing away. He speaks the man's name and he turns. Then the man with the moustache clubs him down, and the big man falls dead.

"The man with the club, the killer, looks to the mine but does not go that way. He gets on his horse and rides away very softly, going into the trees."

"Then what happened?"

"Then Fist, the Mandan, left and he traveled to the bald mountain, where he found a large bull elk and its harem. Fist had only his old musket . . ."

"Another time," Ruff said, and Fist again looked offended.

"It is a good story of how I shot the elk."

"Yes, I know it must be. We will save it for some

night when the winds are cold and we sit around a campfire together."

"If you wish it to be so," the old Indian said stiffly.

"It'll have to be, I'm afraid. I have to travel, Fist."

"To travel!" The Indian laughed and shook his head. "You will not travel far. Fist will have to walk behind you to pick you up when you fall."

"You may be right." Just then Ruff didn't feel that he could walk across the clearing, but he had to do it, had to be moving.

"Where is it you wish to go, Hunter? Back to Bear Fork to tell the sheriff the tale?"

"Yes. Back there. After I make another stop."

Justice was grim; his bloodless, gaunt face was set with determination. The eyes were too bright, staring off into the distance.

"Where?" Fist asked. "Where is it you must first go?"

"Why, to the Morgans' camp, Fist. They tried to kill me. They left me for dead. Now I'm going to crawl back out of my grave and finish the war they started."

9

The Mandan Indian was silent for a long while. He stood there on the windblown ledge staring at the man before him. Ruff Justice was shirtless, the knees of his buckskins torn out. He was extremely pale, leaning against a tree to prop himself up. His chest was bandaged, and Fist knew too well what lay beneath the bandages, an ugly deep wound that had bled much. The Hunter, as he called Ruff Justice, had many abrasions and smaller cuts and bruises. He had struck his head when he fell—perhaps he had struck it too hard and his senses had been jolted.

"What you say is madness."

"Is it?"

"You cannot crawl to where your enemies are."

"And your enemies, Fist."

"And my enemies, but I do not wish to kill them. They cannot find me, and for me to harm them would only bring more whites into the hills. More whites who would either drive Fist away or kill him."

"Do what you wish, then." Justice shrugged, then winced with pain as that slight movement of his shoulders brought back the agony.

Fist smiled gently and moved to Ruff, putting a hand on his shoulder. "I understand that you wish revenge. But is it not better to wait? Wait until you are strong again, then your war will be successful."

"I can't wait, Fist. That's the whole problem. I've got to get back to Bear Fork and see the sheriff."

"Then forget these Morgans!"

Ruff shook his head and fixed his eyes on the Mandan. "No. I don't forget a thing like that—men trying to cut me down."

"If you attempt to fight now, you are doing the job for them. You will surely kill yourself."

"Yes," Ruff agreed. "You're probably correct."

The Indian sighed, his hand slipping from Justice's shoulder. "Then you will go?"

"Yes, I will go."

"What is there for me to do then but to go with you? I have labored patiently to keep you alive. Now you wish to throw your life away. I cannot let you do it—it is up to me, therefore, to go with you, to see that your worthless body is not harmed further."

Ruff smiled and stuck out his hand. Fist took it after a moment's hesitation, shaking his own head as with sadness. "You have brought the spirits of madness to my mountain, Hunter. You have old Fist now ready to enter battle at a time of life when he should be sitting in a comfortable lodge watching his grandchildren play."

"You mentioned a musket. You have a weapon, then?"

"I have my musket, yes. But it is a slow machine, Hunter. Slow to load, slow to fire, but very accurate. These others, these Morgans, they have modern guns."

"Yes. We'll have to plan carefully. How many of them are there?"

"I have seen no more than six."

No more than six. And they had one musket between them—an old Mandan Indian and a crippled, weakened scout. Perhaps Fist was right. Perhaps Ruff had brought the spirits of madness to the mountain. Nevertheless, there was going to be battle, and there would be Morgan blood spilled as well.

"Where is their camp?" Ruff asked. "How is it situated?"

Fist with a defeated sigh began to show Justice all he knew of the Morgans' camp. They had built two cabins in a narrow valley lower down the mountain, toward the plains, which was more convenient for their raiders returning from forays, sufficiently distant from Bear Fork to assure they would be unobserved, near enough for supply runs and whiskey.

They appeared to have chosen their site well. There was a good mile of open grass before the cabins, cliffs rising on two sides, a craggy shoulder of the mountain on the south.

"Difficult to attack," Fist said.

"But you know a way to approach the place."

"I know many ways," Fist said. "But not so many for you. I myself could crawl through the grass. It would take the entire day, but no one would see me until I rose up. You cannot do this. It will have to be down the mountain and into the back of their camp." He looked at Ruff. "It will be very difficult for a man in your condition."

"I expected that. Anything's going to be rough on me just now." But nothing would be quite so rough as forgetting that they had tried to kill him. Justice wasn't willing to do that.

"You will not change your mind?"

"No." Ruff's head swung slowly from side to side. "What's the point in it anyway, Fist? They'll come again if I let them live now. They'll come again and do the job right. Now is the time to retaliate, now while they think me dead."

Fist just nodded. If the man wouldn't change his mind, then it was done. There was no point in talking about it further. The battle had been decided upon; let them plan the battle.

"This is my weapon, the only one I have," Fist said, showing him the Civil War rifle-musket he carried. It wasn't much of a weapon, but those things had killed a lot of men in their time, and used properly, perhaps it would see them through this battle.

"There are a dozen arrows in my quiver. I can make more if there is time."

"There's no time." Besides, if twelve weren't enough, two dozen wouldn't be. That was their total armament, then: bow and arrows, an ancient musket, knives, and a war club that Fist removed carefully from his war bag and turned over fondly.

"Yes," he said, smiling, "this has seen war. I recall . . ." His voice fell away and he shook his head reminiscently.

An hour later they walked from the camp and up a hidden, narrow trail that degenerated into widely spaced toeholds leading up a sheer cliff face. Each time Ruff stretched out his left arm, pain spasmed in his chest. He had to watch carefully where Fist put his hands and toes, otherwise he could not have climbed the rock at all.

As it was, it was torture. His head rang, his stomach was cramped with nausea. Sweat trickled into his eyes. Fist, one hand on an inches-wide outcropping, turned to look down at Ruff.

"It was more difficult with you on my back," the old Indian said. Ruff couldn't even gasp an answer. He had been taken down this way! In the darkness? He had heard it said that Fist climbed like a mountain goat, but he was more than that—he was like a spirit, a moving shadow that needed no grip to hold him to the rocks.

The last few feet Justice wouldn't have made if Fist, seeing that the white man was exhausted, that the blood seeping out from his wound was running down his legs, streaking the gray-white rocks, hadn't leaned over, clamped his hand around Ruff's wrist with incredible strength, and pulled him up onto the shelf. There Justice lay gagging, head throbbing with pain, soaked in his own blood and sweat.

Fist didn't say anything. He simply crouched down, his knees up nearly to his chin, watching—the man would live or he would die. He would make his mad war or they would kill him. It would be the way it was meant to be.

"All right," Ruff said after a while, turning his head to spit out a mouthful of blood and bile. "Help me up, and we'll go on."

Fist said, "I hope I am never your enemy, Hunter." He gave Ruff his hand and helped him to his feet.

They moved on, traveling easier now, down one of those long-forgotten trails carved into the flank of the bald mountain. Ahead Ruff could see timber now, water sheeting over rock glinting in the sunlight. Clouds had crept in from somewhere to smother a portion of the sky to the south. They shone golden-orange at their crests, glowed a dull and menacing blue-purple underneath. Their shadows stained the hills and the plains beyond, which were lost in a murky haze.

"Rain," Fist said, and it puzzled him. He had not smelled this storm coming, and it was moving in from the south, which was very unusual, somehow ominous.

Ruff didn't answer. He couldn't. His mouth was a dry cottony mass. His tongue was a wooden thing cleaving to his palate. His breathing was labored and fiery. He simply trudged on, watching Fist's back, the muscles moving easily under his coppery skin, the deerskin quiver slung across his shoulder.

He ran and he looked to the trees below, hoping against hope they could make it that far without being spotted. If they were seen on that barren slope, a marksman could settle in and pick them off like targets in a shooting gallery.

The pain drifted up and away from Ruff. He trotted along, light-headed and empty. He seemed to be above himself watching his own body. He could see the mountain, the distant plains, the clouds massing to the south, spiked through with lightning.

He was floating more than running. He couldn't remember where he was running just then. He veered to the right, leaving his body behind, running up the sheer slope of the mountain and on. He ran into the sky and watched the tiny world below him, blood-covered, death-scented. There was a black eye watching him from out of a vast fiery void ahead of him, and he ran that way, naked, unafraid, without pain.

"Still. Stay still."

Ruff's eyes blinked open. Something was wrong; he was wet, lying flat on his back. Overhead were trees. "God, it's dark!" He struggled to get up, but Fist placed his hands on his shoulders and held him back. "What happened?"

"You ran as far as you could run and then you fell. I brought you into the trees and you have slept the day away. It was best."

"The Morgans . . ."

"The Morgans will go nowhere. Since you left me in charge, I decided to hold the battle until darkness could cover our approach."

"To let me rest, you mean."

"Yes," Fist said. "Dead men do not fight so very well. You are hungry?"

"Yes." Grumbling unhappily, Ruff sat up. The day had been wasted away. His damned, miserable body had refused to do his work. It had just collapsed, refused to obey an order, and it was infuriating.

He had to admit that he felt better now, stronger.

He sat up to eat, staring at the clouds floating above the tips of the dark pines.

"It rained."

"Yes. There was much thunder and lightning, very little rain. Only enough to cool you."

"We are near their camp?"

"Just above it," Fist said. "I have been twice to look down upon it; they are there—all of them, I believe. No one is out to stand guard. They do not like the rain."

"Good." The Morgans wouldn't post guards. Why should they? Who had they to fear out here? Ruff Justice was supposed to be dead, the law wouldn't chase them into these hills—there was only Sheriff Marks around anyway. Fist? Why should they fear Fist? They saw only an old withered Mandan who had fled from them at first sight. They didn't see the Fist that Ruff Justice saw. Unusually strong, woodswise, with years of battle experience. A man of quiet competence, a ghost when he did not wish to be seen. He was a good ally and, Ruff thought, would make a very dangerous enemy.

Justice got to his feet after eating and drinking. His head was throbbing dully, his chest ached, but he felt much fitter than he had that morning. He was stiff, but as they began to walk and the blood started to move about his body, he limbered up.

It was, as Fist had promised, not far to the Morgans' cabin. The two men emerged from the woods and were able to look down a rocky slope into the secluded valley. They could see a light shining through a window in one cabin. The other was dark. The clouds darkened the night so that this was the only light visible for miles. The stars were screened by shifting, rumbling masses of cloud as the summer storm moved over.

Ruff's breath caught as he saw the way down Fist

had found for them. It was worse than the path up out of his hidden camp. Sheer stone almost unbroken by outcroppings, seams, anything to give a man a handhold. No wonder the Morgans felt secure in their camp. To compound matters, the rock was now rain-slick.

"It is not so bad as it seems," Fist said, but his face betrayed him. It was bad. Especially for a man with one good arm who was subject to passing out from time to time.

The wind twisted through Ruff's long dark hair. He stood bare-chested, shivering in the darkness. He looked far across the convoluted hills, slowly breathing in and out.

"Let's have at it, Fist," he said.

The Indian went first—very cautiously, Ruff noticed. Fist was very good, but the darkness and rain made it treacherous. He eased over the rim at his chosen spot and searched with his foot for a toehold. His head vanished and Justice lowered himself to the ground, cursing himself through clenched teeth as he followed Fist.

It was an hour and a half to the bottom, Justice clinging dizzily to tiny knobs of stone, fingers bloodying themselves as they searched for the smallest cracks, for roots to cling to. At times Fist would reach up and grip Ruff's ankle and guide his foot to a meager toehold. Twice Justice slipped, sliding down the stony face terrifyingly, only to find a saving outcropping, a thumb-sized projection to snatch at, halting his fall.

By the time they reached the bottom Justice was exhausted, and he sagged trembling to the rocky earth. Ahead was a field of large stones that had crumbled off the mountain, forming a sea of gray rocks. Beyond that, just visible, was the light from the cabin window.

A horse whickered from somewhere. Ruff sat breathing deeply, fighting off the dizziness. Whatever they had accomplished to this point was not nearly so great as the task ahead of them.

There were six armed and violent men ahead, murderers all, all well-armed. They brought against them a handful of arrows and a musket.

They had come too far to change their minds, and there was no thought of it in Ruff's mind. He saw now that Fist had opened a small rawhide pouch he had carried tied to his belt. Chanting very softly, a sound like the wind moving through the trees, Fist worked.

He knotted up his hair and tied three feathers into it. His gnarled fingers dipped into the bag, and Ruff saw him smear dark paint across his cheek in three straight lines. His lips were blackened then and a sign of some kind was painted on his chest.

Fist looked up at Ruff and nodded. He rose and offered Justice his choice of weapons. Ruff would have preferred the bow and arrows, but he left these for the man who was undoubtedly a master with them.

He took the musket, a small pouch of powder and shot. Then they moved out across the field of stone toward the enemy who waited ahead.

10

They moved from rock to rock. Ahead the cabins were silent. They might have been deserted but for the lantern light showing through the cabin window. The clouds raced past, lower now, and occasional lightning sparked across the frothing skies.

Ruff eased out of the rocks, forward onto the grass, moving on his belly, the musket cradled in his arms. The pain was still there, but it was distant now as all of his senses concentrated on his objective, prepared themselves for war.

Fist was beside him, silent, painted, grim. He no longer looked so old. His movements were stealthy, fluid. The Mandan stopped and jabbed a finger toward the trees in back of the cabin and Justice nodded, watching as Fist slithered toward them.

He hadn't made the trees when the back door of the cabin popped open.

Justice brought the musket around, realizing how pathetically useless the old weapon was. It would serve a hunter well—a good hunter who could make his first shot count, but reloading would be painfully slow. For Justice, who had not seen one since Cross Keys during the war, it would take a minute at least, although he had been rehearsing things in his mind since he set eyes on the musket.

His eyes were fixed on the man who came out the door, walked through the pool of light cast onto the grass before the door was banged shut behind him, an audible curse sounding from within.

"It's closed, isn't it?" the man outside shouted.

He was big-shouldered, paunchy. He walked to the side of the house and stood looking up at the starless sky as he unbuttoned his fly and leaned a bracing hand against the side of the cabin.

The arrow was silent and deadly. Justice saw it quivering in his back, then saw the big man slowly slump to the ground.

There was a chance—the man had been wearing a gun belt. If Justice could get near enough . . . The cabin door opened again. A second man came out, saw the body, and cried out.

"Hey, something's—" An arrow thudded into his chest and he staggered back into the cabin to fall onto the floor.

"Close that damn door!"

"What in the hell!"

There was a tangle of cursing and shouting. A gun fired, aimed at nothing, and the dead man was dragged into the house, the door slammed shut, the bar falling to audible all the way to where Ruff lay in the long grass, musket in hands.

"We've bought it now," he muttered. There were four of the Morgan gang left. Only four, but armed and barricaded in the cabin. Ruff glanced to where Fist had been, but he could no longer see the Indian. Justice began to make his own move.

His first objective was the second cabin. Fist had the only door to the other covered and they might fire a hundred rounds of ammunition out the window, but they weren't going to hit anything and none of them was going to try coming out—not after seeing two of their men killed.

The second cabin was a different story. Was it empty? Men could have slipped from it already, to circle toward the horses or behind Fist and Ruff.

Justice took a chance and rose from the grass to trot unsteadily through the darkness toward the cabin. Dark yet, still, the door closed, the chimney sending no smoke into the night skies. That, Ruff reminded himself, was all appearance and didn't have anything at all to do with the reality.

He was suddenly there, back pressed against the log wall of the cabin, seeing the flash of firing weapons from the other structure, hearing the boom of the guns, feeling the faint vibration in the wall behind him as the bullets of the Morgan gang sought Fist.

Justice turned, hair hanging in his eyes, hands cold around the cold musket he held.

He stood to one side of the door and waited. He stepped out suddenly and slammed his foot into the door, going down as it banged open, and the load of buckshot from within filled the air over his head, a gout of red and yellow flame from the muzzle of the scattergun blindingly illuminating. Justice saw only the dark silhouette, the rapid movement. He triggered off the musket and saw the man fall, heard the muted howl of pain.

He rolled inside the door, dived toward the body of the dying man, and a pistol cracked from across the room, the bullet thudding into the floor behind Ruff, striking the spot where he had been moments before. He came to his knees, winged the musket across the darkened room, and heard metal clang against metal, heard the strangled oath.

His hands were at the dead man's waist, searching for but not finding a belt gun. Suddenly the second man launched himself across the room and in the darkness collided with Ruff Justice. Ruff felt thumbs searching for his eyes, trying to gouge them from his skull.

Ruff struck out wildly, slamming a forearm into his attacker's face. His chest wound tore free with that movement and blood streamed out as the pain stabbed through his chest.

The outlaw had his hands around Ruff's throat now and Ruff's head was lifted from the floor to be slammed back against it. Instinct caused him to bring the murderous bowie from its sheath, and with a savage exultance he drove it into the outlaw's belly. The twelve-inch blade angled up as Justice buried it to the hilt and the point of it caught heart muscle.

The outlaw convulsed, and enraged as he realized that he was dying, he slammed his fists into Ruff's face, stunning the scout. The lights exploded in Ruff's head, the bells began to ring, and he went out cold beneath the bulk of the Morgan man.

It could have been only seconds, but it seemed like hours, days, until Justice came around again. He lay there not realizing what had happened until he discovered that the difficulty he was experiencing in breathing was due to the two-hundred-pound dead man lying on top of him. With disgust Ruff rolled the man to one side and got to his knees, where he remained shaking his head to clear it.

Gunshots still rang out sporadically from the other cabin. Justice crossed the room and searched the floor with his feet. His toe brushed something solid and he bent over, rising with a satisfied grunt. The Colt felt cool, comforting in his hand.

He hobbled to the doorway, broke open the Colt, and ejected the spent cartridges—bullets spent trying to kill him. Reloading from his belt loops, he started across the grass toward the other cabin, hoping that Fist could identify him in this light, which grew poorer as the clouds bunched again and a light rain fell.

He circled wide, moving cautiously, feeling much

better now, light-headed but alert, his heart pumping evenly, his eyes clear, vision sharp.

He found Fist behind the oak tree still watching the door to the cabin.

"I heard the other fight," the Mandan said.

"Yes. There's only two men in this house," Ruff told Fist. They had killed two each, and that left but two. Of course, there could be a man more and less, but the numbers were approximately even. The Morgans had the advantage as long as they stayed where they were. But had they the patience for that?

Hour by hour Fist and Ruff stayed in the oaks, watching the cabin, from which occasional fire still rang. The clouds, heavy and leaden, sagged past, nearly touching the grass of the high valley, and the rain fell.

"They're not coming out," Justice said.

"Do we leave them?"

"Not hardly," Justice answered grimly.

"Burn them out?"

"It's the only way. Think those walls will catch in this weather?"

"If the fire is hot enough, all things must burn. But I think it is better to use smoke, Ruff Justice."

"Down the chimney?" Justice looked to the stone chimney, considering it. A bullet fired from the cabin came uncomfortably near, whining off the trunk of the big oak, and Justice flinched reflexively.

"It seems the only way if you will not let them escape."

"No, Fist. I won't let them escape."

"Very well. I have flint and steel."

Ruff nodded. He looked again to the chimney. It wouldn't be that difficult in this weather to cross the open space, leap up and grab the eaves, and work across to the chimney. Then a bundle of wet leaves or grass down the spout.

"Give me the flint."

"This is a job for me," Fist said with a smile. "I can still climb—you pretend to climb."

"All right," Justice said. "Go on, then."

He saw Fist sift off through the low clouds, the darkness, saw him collecting something from the ground as he went; then Fist was gone. A minute later he saw a figure leap toward the eaves on the side of the house and swing gracefully up. A bundle was pulled up after him. Fist walked the ridge pole then, his silhouette stark against a patch of clear sky.

Inside the cabin they knew what was coming. Bullets started punching holes through the sod roof. A dozen, two dozen of them, breaking off only when the guns needed to be reloaded.

It didn't do any good. Fist was to the chimney. Ruff saw the tinder catch, then saw the flames begin to gnaw at the damp material Fist had gathered. Then he saw no flames as the bundle was lowered partway down the chimney.

Fist was back in ten minutes to lie beside Ruff watching the door.

"It went out," Ruff said. "They got it out or it went out."

"Wait. Use patience."

"There's not enough downdraft."

"Wait, my friend. Are you always in so much of a hurry?"

It was then that the unexpected occurred, upsetting the whole apple cart. From down the valley they heard the approach of hoofbeats. First with disbelief, then with anger, Justice listened, his eyes searching the cloud banks until the shadowy horsemen began to appear one by one. There were three of them, all wearing yellow rain slickers that stood out vividly against the prevailing gloom.

Fist inhaled sharply through his teeth. Mounted men were a different story. They had the advantage, and Ruff and Fist had left themselves no way out of that valley.

"What do we do?" Fist asked.

Before Justice could answer, the door to the cabin burst open, and behind a rolling cloud of smoke two outlaws appeared, one with a gun in each hand, blazing away as the newcomers, startled, their horses rearing, drew their weapons.

"Over there, damn you, Harry!" the man with two guns roared out, and the horsemen, in some confusion, started forward.

"We're not going to outrun them," Justice said. Fist was already notching an arrow. Justice took steady aim with the Colt he had picked up in the cabin and shot the first rider from his mount.

At that the other outlaws opened up with a savage barrage, four weapons firing rapidly, all aimed at Justice's muzzle flash, tearing chunks of wood from the old oak, plowing up the earth around Justice and Fist.

Ruff brought up the Colt with two hands, patiently sighted, and squeezed off, seeing another outlaw fall from his horse to be dragged by his panicked horse through the night and clouds.

That left three of them and a minute later there were only two. A recklessly charging gunman took an arrow in the throat, stood up in his stirrups, and toppled to the earth.

Ruff saw that only from the corner of his eye. The man he had his sights on was the big man with two guns. He was now backing toward the corner of the cabin, screened momentarily by a bewildered horse that was stepping on its own reins as it tried to get away from the roar of sound, the folly of men.

He was a big man, Ruff had noticed immediately, and he wore a black beard. He was a Morgan, either Art or Jake. Ruff wanted him—he wanted to end the threat of the Morgan gang once and for all, and he thought he had the old bull in his sights.

Suddenly the horse was gone and so was Morgan.

Justice got to his feet, cursing, firing after the horse. He could see Morgan now clinging to the side of the animal, vanishing into the clouds. The second man had remained behind and now his covering fire drove Ruff diving back behind the tree.

In another moment there was no sound at all in the valley. It was eerie, inexplicable, until Justice peered out and saw the last man flat on his back, his hand clenching the arrow that pierced his heart.

Lightning chose that moment to strike close at hand and the battlefield was lighted to momentary whiteness. The rain began to fall in earnest and Ruff Justice walked from cover, Fist beside him, his painted face grim.

They examined the dead. Ruff knew none of them outside or within the first cabin. When they returned to the second cabin, however, and lit the lantern there, he saw who his attacker had been.

Art Morgan lay dead on the floor, his beard matted, stained with his own blood.

"We must not stay here. Perhaps their leader will return with more warriors."

"You're right." There may have been loot hidden around the place, but the sheriff would have to search for it—if he was inclined to.

Now that the fighting was done, Ruff's pain returned with heavy insistence. He felt exhausted. He would have liked to lie down and sleep on the wet grass with the dead.

They managed to find two horses, and as the rain battered the world, the thunder rolling down the long canyon, they rode from the place. Neither talked for a long while; perhaps Fist shared Ruff's emotions.

Now that the outlaws were dead, he felt no exultation. It was something that had to be done, but there was no pleasure involved in seeing them lie there, the rain washing down over their lifeless bodies. Hell, someone, somewhere, must have cared about them, such as they were. And one day—Justice knew this as surely as he knew he had been born—he would be lying there, his guts torn open, his heart stopped by a flying slug of remorseless lead.

"Now," Fist said as they came out of the valley and onto the Bear Fork creek road, "I must go. You have placed me under a spell, Hunter. I should not have made war. Now they will drive me from these hills or murder me. I cannot stay."

"I want you to talk to the sheriff."

"No."

"I won't let him hold you."

"No. If he sees me, he will arrest me. My word will do no good. This you have said yourself. Do not force me to do anything, Hunter—or try to force me. We have been friends, fellow warriors. Let us part as friends."

"To save a man's life, Fist."

"A man I do not know."

"That is so. You don't know him or his wife, who will have to carry on alone somehow, living under a cloud of shame." Ruff looked deliberately away from Fist. "You don't know what it is to be ashamed, to be shunned by your own people, do you, Fist?"

"Ah, Justice, you are heartless. Yes . . . I was shunned, but I have told you I was falsely accused."

"Yes?"

"As this man is. I know. But what do I owe him, Hunter? I cannot let the sheriff see me."

"Then you'll talk to him without him seeing you."

"How can this be done?"

"If it can be, will you do it?"

The rain slanted down, the wind twisted past them,

lifting Ruff's hair, the mane of the horse he rode. Fist hissed in frustration and at last said, "Yes! If I do not have to see him. I will not go to a white jail. If I am jailed, I shall never forgive you, Hunter. I shall curse your soul for eternity. I shall . . ."

"Come along. Let's get going," Ruff said, and it was a good thing that it was dark so that the old Mandan couldn't see the grin on Justice's face. "Ride lightly," he reminded Fist. "We've still got us a Morgan out here."

A Morgan and Bull Bromfield and all of his people, Jack Sagan and the sheriff. The darkness and the rain cloaked them in invisibility, making the long ride into town miserable. Still, Justice was pleased with the turn the weather had taken. He wasn't ready yet to meet Bromfield or anyone else who had a stake in stopping Ruff Justice. And they would try again, Ruff knew. There was too much at stake—a fortune, enough to last a man several lifetimes. All of the mineral wealth in the three claims.

Sagan and Bromfield had staked everything on that. If they lost, their reward would be a rope around the neck or a bullet. They weren't about to let one man in buckskins stop them now.

11

Sheriff Marks' eyes flickered open in the darkness. Alf Marks had run into trouble in his time—on both sides of a badge. He had been run out of Abilene for bottom-dealing, been tarred and feathered for altering brands in El Paso. Deciding that the side of righteousness was having all the fun, he had accepted a town marshal's badge in Schooner, Wyoming, and for half a year lived comfortably until the town died, having failed to obtain the railroad spur it had hoped for. Marks had moved on, taking two other jobs on the strength of his Schooner experience, both in hardscrabble mining towns that had perished as the ore went. On occasion he had helped himself to funds left unattended, but he also prided himself on the fact that he, acting alone, had taken down the Frazee brothers, wanted men. The fact that he had gotten both of them from a rooftop with his rifle didn't disturb him any more than it had bothered the citizens of the town. They had just wanted to get rid of the Frazees, who had the habit of burning down towns when they tired of them.

Marks had run into trouble in his time—and he had been scared. But there is nothing like awakening in the dead of night to the ratcheting of a pistol, to feel the nudge of cold steel against your temple, to drive fear like an iron stake through your heart.

"What is it?" Marks asked in panic. He lay utterly still, his heart thudding against the bars of his rib cage. He could see absolutely nothing. The room was completely dark. Outside, he could hear rain pattering down.

"Just hold still and nothing's going to happen."

The voice was deep, disguised, but it was somehow familiar to the sheriff. He didn't waste much time trying to identify it. He was more concerned with staying alive, just staying alive.

Marks had seen what a .44 bullet can do to a man's skull—explode it like a melon—and he had enough imagination to be able to see his own head destroyed like that. He didn't move an eyebrow. Cold sweat ran down from his forehead, trickled past his ear, and spotted his dingy pillowcase.

"What do you want?" he croaked. "My roll's over there in the bureau. Fifteen hundred dollars—take it."

"I don't want your money."

"What, then?"

The man with the gun didn't answer. He was backing away from Marks now, moving toward the window.

"What's happening? Don't kill me, for God's sake!"

Again there was no answer. Marks saw the man raise the sash and he felt the damp wind blow into the room. A second man had appeared, only a dark silhouette beyond the window, faceless and menacing.

"What is this?"

"Be quiet. I want you to hear something. Now you lie there and listen."

"Sure. All right. Go ahead," Marks agreed anxiously.

"Tell him," the man with the gun said.

"Harlan Busby did not kill his partner. I was there. I saw it. The man who killed him was very big, with a moustache. He rides a pale horse and carries a club with him."

The voice was accented, Marks noticed. What kind

of accent? Sure—an Indian. It had to be Fist, then, didn't it? Yes, Fist! Then the man with the gun was Justice. Or was it? Marks was suddenly confused by the darkness, the whine of the wind, his own fear.

A man with a moustache, a big man, one who carried a club with him. That was Bull Bromfield. He carried a club all the time. He had busted a few heads with it, too. Ask those miners of his. You didn't get out of line on an Amalgamated job. Not with Bull Bromfield around. But they hadn't told him that Bull had done the job on Blakely. . . . Marks' grasping mind began to work on that. What could be made out of this? He could, he supposed, earn himself a grave if he wasn't careful, but if a man went about it right . . .

"Are you listening, Marks?"

"Yes."

"All right," the man with the gun said. Who was that? It had to be Justice, or he thought it had to be, but they said that Morgan had finished Justice off up on the bald mountain. "Listen now. Sam Settle was killed with a club as well. Bull Bromfield killed both men."

"I can't do anything . . ."

"That's right. You can't do anything, you won't do anything. You're a coward, Marks. You've got your star pinned to Jack Sagan's coattails. Let me tell you this right now—Sagan's going to lose. You'll make nothing out of this.

"And remember, this can happen again. A man that can come up on you one night can do it again. Maybe next time it won't be just to talk. You think about that, Marks. Then you do what you think you have to do."

The man with the gun backed away from Marks and he saw him throw a leg up over the sill and go out into the alley. Still Marks didn't rise for a long while. He lay there feeling the wind rush over him, cooling the sweat.

"Now what the hell do I do?" Marks asked himself. Cross Sagan? Not likely. Wait for the man with the gun to come back? All in all, California sounded like a good idea, but Marks had too much tied up in Bear Fork. A fortune, Sagan had promised him, if he stayed on the right side.

And if it wasn't the right side . . . Marks was just liable to find himself swinging by the neck beside Sagan and Bull Bromfield. The sheriff didn't sleep well the rest of that night.

Nor did Amy Settle.

She heard the tap at her door and she tumbled from the bed, yawning, blinking, staring at the darkness. The tapping became more insistent and she padded toward the door, the floor cool against her bare feet, her nightdress doing little to keep her warm.

She opened the door and Ruff Justice stumbled in and fell against her.

"Sorry." He clung to her, smiling sheepishly.

"Oh, Ruff, what's happened to you?"

"I'm all right. Just about healed up . . ." Then he went out, and if Amy hadn't caught him, he would have hit the floor.

She dragged him to her bed, returned to lock the outer door and the connecting door to Mrs. Busby's room, then lit the lamp at her bedside.

She was shocked at his appearance, shocked and saddened. His face was gaunt and pale, sunken. Dried blood seemed to cake the entire upper half of his body, and when she got most of that washed away, she found the filthy bandage underneath.

"I should get a doctor. They've got one in Bear Fork." Amy looked to the door and then back to the unconscious man. "Maybe you don't want me to let anyone know you're here. Oh, Ruff! Darn you, what do you want me to do?"

She decided to look to the wound herself first. It

wasn't bleeding now. His pulse was strong. Perhaps he was simply exhausted. Who, she wondered, had put the bandage on?

There was a tapping at the connecting door and Amy's head jerked up.

"Is everything all right, dear?" Mrs. Busby called softly. "I saw your light on . . ."

"Yes, yes. I just can't sleep. Is the light disturbing you?"

"No," Emily Busby said, a faint questioning in her voice. "I just didn't know what was happening. I'll go back to sleep."

Amy continued to watch the door. Why, she didn't know. She certainly could trust Emily Busby—but lately it had been best not to trust a soul.

She finished removing the bandage, saw the yellow-white poultice beneath it, and began washing it away. The wound, when it became visible, was red, puckered, nasty-looking, but she didn't think dangerous, unless a man got blood poisoning—a very real possibility.

A doctor, then, or not? She couldn't decide and she jabbed her fingers into her disheveled golden hair in annoyance.

"What could the doctor do?" she asked herself. Disinfectant and perhaps stitches. Well, she could do that as well. She had a general store right across the street. She could purchase a bottle of carbolic, needle and thread—then, if they were looking for Justice, she wouldn't be helping them.

"Oh, Ruff, I hope I'm doing the right thing."

Gently she undressed him. His buckskin trousers were torn open at the knees, and those knees were slashed too—by stones, it seemed. She tossed the pants in the corner and went to get the washbasin and pitcher. She stood looking at him, naked, lean, helpless on her bed, and she smiled; then, wiping the hair from her eyes, she got busy washing him down, covering him with the sheet when she was finished.

He had a Colt revolver in his holster. It didn't, she noticed, seem to be the one he had had before, and Amy lifted the gun from it and pulled a chair nearer to the bed.

Outside, it was still raining lightly, and wrapping a blanket around her shoulders, the Colt in her lap, she blew out the lamp and sat watch through the early-morning hours, watching the rain streak the window, listening to the wind of the summer storm while Ruff Justice breathed shallowly, sleeping the time away, appearing completely at peace, all of his pain temporarily banished.

She was there still when dawn broke, golden-orange bands of light streaming through the dissipating clouds. At eight, when the general store opened, she left, locking the door behind her, leaving the pistol near Ruff's right hand.

She tapped on Mrs. Busby's door.

"I won't be going to breakfast this morning, Emily."

There was a momentary puzzled silence from within. "All right, dear. I'll eat and then go visit Harlan."

"Fine. I'll see you later, then."

That settled, Amy marched down the stairs and through the lobby. She stepped outside and practically walked into Bull Bromfield.

"Well, Miss Settle," the big man said, touching his hat brim in what was, with him, a mocking gesture. "Have you thought things over?"

"I won't sell the mine."

"Then you'll lose it, won't you?"

"Perhaps."

"A woman without money in this country is in for a hard time. You ought to think twice. Or are you expecting that Justice to help you out of this?" He was smiling, a dirty smile, as if he knew something Amy didn't.

It came to her suddenly. Bull Bromfield knew Justice was hurt—no, he thought him to be dead!

"You hear me," Bromfield said, rocking back on his heels, his thumbs now hooked into his vest pockets. "A woman in this country has to think about what might happen if she hasn't any money to get along on." Then he started laughing, and Amy, her ears burning, walked away, her back rigid.

She walked past the general store; then, glancing back to see that Bromfield had gone into the bank, she spun on her heel and went back.

With carbolic and needle and thread in her purse she went back to the hotel, quickly up the stairs and back into the room.

He lay there propped up on a pillow looking at her with dancing blue eyes.

"Ruff!" There was something approaching dismay in her voice and he grinned.

"What's the matter?"

"I thought you'd still be unconscious." She walked nearer to the bed and then sat down, his hand running up her arm.

"You like me down and out?"

"I wanted to do some doctoring. I'm afraid I'll hurt you if you're awake."

"Yes, you likely will. What did you have in mind?"

She showed him the carbolic and the needle, which now looked inordinately large.

"And what's that, sailmaker's thread?" he gibed.

Amy blushed and then her temper began to rise. "Only kidding, lady." Ruff Justice pulled her down to him and kissed her. She went slack across his body, her eyes softened.

"Now you see why I wanted you unconscious," she breathed. Her fingers ran along his eyebrows, down his cheek to his lips, which she kissed tenderly, searchingly.

"You'd better get to your work," he said, patting her rump.

"You're going to let me doctor you anyway?"

"It's you or some sawbones. That thing won't stay closed up. It needs sewn."

"It would stay closed up if you'd stay down and let it."

"Can't. There's been a lot to do, more to be done yet."

"I saw Bull Bromfield. He's gloating already. Why wouldn't he?" she asked reflectively. "I've got exactly three days, you know that?"

"A lot can happen in three days." Ruff tensed slightly as he saw Amy pour a huge dollop of carbolic on a cloth pad. "That stuff burns like hell, you know."

"Yes."

She got to it, and Ruff, who had had carbolic dabbed on various parts of his body too many times to count, discovered that his recollections of the stuff were all too accurate. It burned his nostrils, seared the open wound. His eyes watered as he looked up into the concerned face of his nurse.

"That," she said finally, "is the easy part. It's usual to drink some whiskey, I suppose."

"I don't drink," Justice said, regretting that for one of the few times in his life.

"Excuse me?"

"I said I don't drink."

"Oh. Well, you don't hear that much out here. That's what I thought you said," she added as she threaded the silvery needle. "This is not going to feel too good."

It didn't. Amy, sucking and biting at her lip, speaking to herself as she worked, stitched him up like a prize quilt. They were both relieved when she was finished.

"Now, then?" she asked him.

"Now, then—food. A lot of food."

"All right." She started away from the bed and Justice grabbed her hand.

"Afterward."

"Afterward?" She sank beside him, a smile growing at the corners of her mouth.

"Yes." He drew her down again, and his kiss this time was more than a greeting. She looked down at him in amazement, then without a word rose and stepped from her clothes. She stood before the window, and the sunlight streaming in painted her to a rich golden hue. Ruff's eyes swept up her ankles, across slender tapered calves to strong, flaring hips and buttocks, lingering on the patch of golden down at the juncture of her thighs. The sunlight danced in her eyes, sunlight and pleasure. Her breasts were firm, the pink nipples standing taut, inviting. Ruff stretched out a hand and she walked slowly toward him, throwing back the sheet, and Amy stood over him for a minute, watching his erection grow as his eyes combed her, as his hand ran up her smooth flank, circled her waist, and drew her nearer.

"This isn't going to work out real well, Ruff. You can't do much moving around."

"We'll figure it out," he said.

Amy bent her head to his abdomen. Her lips danced across it, found their way to his inner thigh and down to his knees. She rose them, straddling him on the bed, her hands finding his erection, circling it, moving inflamingly up his shaft as her eyes met his.

She scooted up farther and Ruff's fingers dropped between her legs to caress the soft skin there, to dip inside and stroke the tender flesh. Amy quivered and slid herself forward still more to sit across his shaft, to slide herself against him, her fingers meeting Ruff's, touching him and herself.

Her head was thrown back, her breasts standing out proud and firm. Justice reached out and found them, his thumbs moving across her taut nipples, and again she shuddered.

Amy lifted herself, raising one knee slightly and then the other as she crouched over him. "I don't want to tear anything loose . . . my best doctoring work to date," she said, her voice breathy, deep.

"Worry about it later," Justice said. His hands encircled her buttocks now, feeling the lithe muscle beneath the sleek feminine flesh, feeling her quiver as she eased forward, grasped his erection, and touched it to herself, gently working the head of it back and forth along the moist slot before she settled on him a bare inch and hovered there, trembling from head to toe, her inner muscles moving, grasping.

Then with a shudder, a sigh, a deep, throaty moan, she settled herself on him, letting him slip into her depths as she bit at her lip and Ruff's hands tightened their grip on her buttocks.

She sat against him, quivering, her heat encircling Ruff, teasing, demanding. Then at last she began to move slowly, dreamily, lifting herself an inch at a time until she again had only the head of his shaft within her, hovering there, poised and trembling, to lower herself slowly until their pelvises met.

Her hand went behind her back to drop and find his sack, to press it against her warm flesh as if she would take that inside too, and she began to pitch and roll, to quake against him moving up and down with uncontrolled eagerness, and Ruff lay back, watching her, his eyes narrowed, seeing the tense need on her face, the blank, distant joy in her eyes as she worked her body into a frenzy of delight and wanting. Then Amy suddenly came undone, grinding herself against him, fluid and warm, her breath coming in gasps, her body tensing, slackening, tensing again as Ruff's own need began to rise and he arched his back, lifting her from her knees.

His hands went between her thighs to spread her, to touch her as he drove it home time and again, Amy's face astonished, drained, radiant in turn as he tortured her with pleasure until he reached a sudden hard climax of his own. She went completely slack, balanced against him, her thighs spread wide, her body drained, her head lolling, her pleasure complete.

Ruff slept deeply then, his consciousness surrendering to a deep abyss, his exhausted body needing, coveting the sleep. When he came around again, she was there, still naked, and at the bedside was a tray of food.

"Hope you didn't go out like that to fetch those vittles."

"No." She laughed. "Would that bother you?"

"Of course. Every man is jealous, no matter what they might claim. A man can be jealous of a woman he's never met. Maybe we're meant to be like bull elks, territorial. Our harem is ours, and that includes every female in it. But I'm especially jealous of you, just now," he added.

"Yes," she said, smiling, "I'll bet. I think you just put that last bit in to salve my feelings."

"What's to eat?"

"Have a look. It doesn't bother you if I sit around like this, does it?"

"Not a bit. It's a little distracting, but I'll manage."

He did manage. He managed through four eggs and two thick slices of ham, grits, potatoes, and coffee. Then he couldn't manage any more and he threw off the sheets once more, and Amy, smiling, came to him again, searching his body with fingers and lips until Ruff fell off into a second exhausted sleep that lasted until nightfall.

12

Amy, soft and warm, was in his arms when he awoke to the sounds in the streets. At first he thought it was gunfire and he rolled from the bed, pistol in hand, seeing Amy sit up, clawing at her sleepy eyes.

"What . . . ?"

Justice shook his head and walked to the window. There were dozens of men in the streets and just now they were amusing themselves by throwing firecrackers under passing horses.

"The Fourth," Ruff muttered wearily. He sat down on a chair to peer at Amy in the half-darkness. "They're getting warmed up for the holiday. Trying to see if they can stay drunk and stay on their feet for two whole days."

Amy didn't answer. She was lost behind an awesome yawn. The sheet had fallen away from her and she sat there like some naked, sated lioness, just as sleek and strong, much more beautiful.

"What are we going to do, Ruff? Nothing's been accomplished, has it? Not really. You eliminated a few more of the Morgans, but that's hardly what you came here to do. You took Fist to the sheriff, but his word carried no weight and you know it. Harlan Busby is still in jail, waiting to hang. I'm still short my thousand dollars. Grant Danziger is still out there risking his neck . . . and Sagan still has all the cards."

"Bull Bromfield is still walking the streets scot-free, although we know he committed double murder," Justice said, completing the unhappy canon. "Yes, I know it. And time's running out."

"So?" She looked to him without much optimism. "What's next?"

"First," he said with a smile, "I suppose I'd better get some clothing. You've held me prisoner long enough."

"Yes, I have!" She laughed. "Poor man." Amy went to him, kissed the nape of his neck, and wrapped her arms around him. "How are you feeling, really?"

"I'm as fit as I hope I'll have to be," was all Justice could tell her. He was, he guessed, half what he should have been, maybe as much as 75 percent. No more. "Hand me my boots, will you?"

There wasn't much left in the boot, but there was gold enough to buy a new outfit. He told Amy as well as he could what he wanted, what size.

"I want a rifle too, Amy. A Spencer fifty-six, and make sure it's a new one. Peer down the bore and . . ."

"I've been around guns, Ruff," she said.

"Okay. A box of cartridges as well."

"Of course." She was dressing now, tugging up a petticoat. She was pretty, damned pretty, Justice decided as she finished buttoning the navy-blue dress she wore and tucked her hair into a matching bonnet.

"You watch yourself, Amy. Those miners are getting themselves worked up."

"Jealous again?"

"You bet."

"They won't bother a woman on Main Street, Ruff. I'll be back as quickly as I can. Then we can go out and eat?" she asked hopefully.

"Yes. Later. First I want to see Sheriff Marks and

see if I've made any impression on him." That reminded him to ask, "How's Emily Busby holding up."

"She's trying," was all Amy could tell him.

She got on tiptoes, kissed him, and went out, her heels clicking on the wooden floor as she walked down the corridor to the stairway. Justice closed the door and went to stand before the window, naked, hands clasped behind him. Yes, they were heating up down there. These men worked hard and they felt they had to play hard. Maybe they simply couldn't relax without the help of alcohol. Long hours underground in brutal heat and a suffocating atmosphere knotted a man up mentally and physically. If there were any men who as a group worked harder, Justice didn't know who they were. A cowboy's life was a dream compared to hard-rock mining.

He walked to the mirror and peered at himself by the faint light of the flickering lantern. He needed a shave but his razor was wherever the little roan had gotten to when Morgan shot him from it. He decided to have at it with the skinning knife.

It wasn't the closest shave he had ever had, but he judged it adequate, and when he was finished, wiping off the soap, he flung himself back on the bed to lie there, hands behind his head, feeling much cleaner and quite satisfied with himself until thoughts of how little he had actually accomplished in Bear Fork began to return and he fell to silent brooding.

"Good evening, Miss Settle."

"Hello, Charlie," she said with a smile. The storekeeper was busy on this evening. The miners had been paid, it was a holiday weekend, the people from the outlying areas had crowded into Bear Fork, lonely prospectors from as far away as Poet Creek. John Schick and his wife had come in from Johnstown; Grant Danziger had abandoned his digs for the spectacle Bear Fork was promising. Fireworks, horse races, even a hanging to cap off the entertainment. Outside, Amy Settle had seen the gallows being constructed by torchlight—and she was sure Harlan Busby could see it from his cell window.

"Be with you in a minute, please," the storekeeper said.

"That's all right, Charlie, I'm in no great hurry."

Across the store Amy saw the sheriff's deputy, Hawkes, idling in his usual corner. She turned deliberately away from him and went to the new bales of black jeans in the corner away from Hawkes, searching through them until she found some trousers long enough for Ruff Justice. She left them on top of the near bale and crossed to where the shirts were, selecting a dark-blue shirt with pearl buttons—maybe Ruff wouldn't like the buttons, but he might as well look fine. Or should he? She deliberated, held the shirt up, put it down, and traded it at last for a maroon shirt with plain black buttons.

"Very nice, Miss Settle," Charlie said at her shoulder, startling her so that she jerked around like a discovered shoplifter.

"I'll take this," she said hurriedly, "and a pair of jeans over there."

Charlie frowned, exchanged that expression for a smile, and walked along with Amy Settle as she picked out some long cotton socks and a fancy scarf. Who, Charlie wondered, is she buying these for? Old man Settle was dead, and he was never that size anyway.

"I'd also like to see a rifle, Charlie. My old Henry's not much anymore."

"Winchester, I suppose . . ."

"That Spencer, please."

"The Spencer? Big weapon, Miss Amy. Terrible kick to a fifty-six, you know. Too much for you. That's a buffalo gun or a war gun, no good for game shooting, to my mind."

"And a box of cartridges. Fifty rounds, I suppose they come in."

"Yes, Miss Amy," Charlie said. He was puzzled, but the customer was always right.

Deputy Hawkes, slowly munching on a purloined cracker, wasn't puzzled at all. He saw it as clear as dawn, and when Amy Settle bought a wide-brimmed doe-colored hat and paid for the lot with double eagles when she hadn't seen cash money in months, he knew positively. Hawkes slid out the door and into the noisy street.

"What's your hurry?"

"Huh?" Hawkes had nearly walked into the banker and now he straightened up, blinking stupidly at Jack Sagan. "Nothing, Mister Sagan. I got to tell the sheriff something."

"Important?" Sagan asked, casually lighting a cigar, sparing a glance for two drunken miners who were riding past on a mule, one of them facing front, the other back.

"It's just that Ruffin Justice fellah—Sheriff thought he was dead. He ain't. I just seen Amy Settle buying a man's kit, down to a big old fifty-six Spencer."

"The sheriff doesn't want Justice for anything, does he?"

"Not nothin' specific, you might say," Hawkes admitted, "but he'd surely like to be able to keep an eye on him."

"Yes." Sagan knew that—those had been his orders to Sheriff Marks. "I believe he's over at the Whiskey Well."

"Yes, sir." Hawkes smiled crookedly. Where else would Sheriff Marks be?

Jack Sagan stepped out of Hawkes' way and onto the plankwalk, where he stood sourly surveying the "rabble" that had taken over the streets. From the shadow of the porch awning he watched as Amy Settle emerged from the store and started back up the street. There was no mistaking the long package wrapped in white paper she carried. So Jake Morgan had been mistaken when he said Justice was dead. And just where the hell was Jake? All of that crowd should have been in town by now. No matter—there was plenty of men who would be willing to do the job he had in mind.

Ruff Justice, dressed and shaven, looked like a whole man again. He wasn't quite, but if you didn't know he was in pain, weak from loss of blood yet, you wouldn't have guessed it.

He looked fine to Amy Settle as she studied him from the bed where she sat. The jeans were an inch too short, but the maroon shirt fit fine, the hat she had bought seemed to suit him. He slung his gun belt around his waist and buckled it up.

"Well?" He turned around, spreading his arms for inspection.

"You'll do, Mister Morgan."

"You didn't see Marks, did you?"

"No, but Hawkes saw me and by now the sheriff is probably expecting you. He'll be at the old stand anyway."

"What do they call it? Whiskey Well?" Amy nodded and Justice walked to her and sat beside her for a moment, kissing her neck beneath the veil of golden hair. "I'll see Marks and then we'll eat. Meet you in the hotel restaurant?"

"Yes. I'll wash and change."

"I'd rather help you do that than talk to the sheriff, but . . ." He looked to the connected room where from time to time they heard the quiet sobbing of Emily Busby.

"Yes. I know. You have to do something, though I don't know what. What *can* you do, Ruff?"

"We'll see." What was needed was a lawyer, not a rough country scout who was good with a knife and gun, good at reading sign and smelling Sioux, but helpless against the machinery of the law. "Maybe he's thought it over by now."

"Sheriff Marks doesn't think," Amy said accurately. "He's told what he's supposed to think."

"Sagan."

"Yes, and you'll not change Jack Sagan's mind."

"No? Maybe not. We'll see, Amy." He rose and started toward the door. "We'll just have to see."

He went out into the hallway before he could be tempted to stay behind with Amy, to forget temporarily all of this mess that he wasn't responsible for but that he seemed to have brought to a head, all of this mess for which there seemed to be no solution.

He found a back door at the end of the corridor, peered out, and saw an outside wooden staircase leading down to the alley below.

Ruff opened the recalcitrant door and went out, surprised at the warmth of the evening. Summer was here finally. There was a lot of uproar downtown, an occasional explosion. With all the fireworks around, he reflected, no one would pay much attention to a gunshot.

He walked silently down the railless staircase and stood for a moment in the alley, seeing nothing but the trash piled high behind the slaughterhouse and the freight office, which were ahead of him, both on his left hand.

He started that way. He had taken three steps when the dark bulky shadows emerged from behind the debris to block his way. Behind him Ruff could hear the sounds of approaching, hurried footsteps. He glanced across his shoulder, saw that there were two more of them coming, and started forward again.

"Evening, gentlemen," Ruff said.

"Evening yourself, dude," the man on Justice's left said sarcastically. He had a club dangling from his hand. Faceless in the shadows, he was huge, blocky.

He lifted the club and charged in, astonishing Justice. He wasn't so astonished that he couldn't step to the side against the wall of the freight office, draw his Colt, and shoot the onrushing thug through the foot.

The man went down with a howl as the echo from the pistol shot racketed up the alleyway. Justice turned back toward the two men behind him, but they had already taken to their heels, as had the third man.

"Amateurs," Ruff growled, walking forward to stand over the injured miner, who lay there rolling around the ground holding his foot. "How much did you get for this?"

"I'll never be able to walk again!"

"Oh, you'll manage. It'll be a little slow, but you'll manage," Justice said, seeing the still-smoldering hole in the miner's boot, the puddle of blood leaking out to stain the ground. "Who sent you? Bromfield or Sagan?"

"Go to hell."

"You're a lucky man, my friend," Justice told him in all seriousness. Lucky, indeed. Ruff should have taken him dead-center. He had the right, but he had seen what he faced. Drunks out to pick up a little loose change. Dumb enough or intoxicated enough to believe they were going to take an armed man with their clubs. All he got for this observation was a pain-ridden curse.

"I'll never walk again. I'll be off work for a month."

He was breaking Ruff's heart. Justice holstered his pistol and walked off up the alley, followed by a stream of abuse. Marks, peculiarly enough, wasn't in the Whiskey Well when Justice looked in there, and he started toward the sheriff's office, the last place people expected to find Marks.

He had nearly made it there when he saw, across the street nearly hidden in the shadows, a lean, familiar figure. Justice started that way, but his way was blocked by a wagon rumbling down Main Street at a tremendous pace, and when the wagon had passed, the man had vanished.

Frowning, Ruff stood there for a minute staring at the head of the alley. He could have sworn that it was Fist, but why would Fist be in this town he despised so much? And why would he have taken to his heels upon seeing Ruff Justice?

Maybe, Justice thought, he was mistaken, but it puzzled him all the same.

He found Marks behind his desk, bleary-eyed, limp, as if exhausted by a long labor.

"Been losing sleep, Marks?" Justice asked, and the sheriff came bolt upright.

"Damn you, Justice!"

"Then you remember me?"

"Remember you? Why, you damned bandit, of course I remember a man who sneaks into my room at night and sticks a gun to my head."

"I guess you don't remember me," Justice said, seating himself on a corner of Marks' desk, putting his hat beside him. "You seem to have me confused with someone else."

"Yes, I do," Marks said, his eyes squinting out from under sandy eyebrows. "And maybe one day I'll have you confused with someone who needs shooting."

"Could be. Maybe that works both ways," Ruff said, and he was smiling, but Marks didn't mistake the steel behind the remark. "There's a rumor that you've come on some new evidence that might warrant a new trial for Harlan Busby."

"Is there? How the hell did you hear that?"

"Don't know. Picked it up somewhere. Any truth to it?"

"Not a damned bit," Marks said savagely.

"No?" Justice looked toward the cell where Harlan Busby slept or perhaps stood at the window staring out at the scaffolding being built for him. "You know, Marks, I can't think of a thing much worse than this: letting a man suffer and die when you know he's innocent."

"I don't know any such thing."

"All right. But you suspect it."

"And if I do? I'm not judge and jury. I can't let a man go free. You think I can do that just to please you?"

"There's a witness, I hear."

"Is there? And just where is he, Justice? Let him come in here and sign a statement, then."

Where was he, indeed? Lurking in alleyways in Bear Fork? Besides, what good would Fist's deposition be? It angered Ruff, frustrated him. He knew in his guts that Harlan Busby was innocent, that Bull Bromfield had done the murders, yet there wasn't a way in the world to prove it. There was nothing to be done about it, nothing at all. And Harlan Busby was going to hang in the morning.

"You want to see the prisoner?" Marks asked.

"No. No, I guess not." See him to tell him that it was all over, that there was no hope left?

"Then maybe you'd better clear out," the sheriff said, rubbing his eyes tiredly. "Listen, Justice, before you go, I'll tell you how it is. I'm not a great lawman, maybe I ain't even much of a man, but seeing Harlan hang is not something I want."

"Then . . ."

"Just a minute." Marks held up a hand. "You know as well as I do how things work around here. Sagan and Bromfield run things. Maybe if I stay with them,

I make out all right in the end. If I don't, well, I'm out of office and back on the trail again . . . at the best.

"Say I up and asked for a new trial, which a law officer in this territory is allowed to do. All right, then, what? We bring forward a series of allegations and suspicions that maybe Bull Bromfield did this—we can't prove it, haven't a chance of him admitting it—where does that leave me when some phantom witness refuses to come forward and I'm relying on hearsay? Why, a decent lawyer would have me hung out to dry. If the witness, say, could come forward, what, then? Say he's the kind of man whose word don't carry no weight with a Western jury. Then the trial's lost anyway. You show me a jury that don't come in with prejudice. Of course they got prejudice; we all do, if we're human. No, Justice, this is a rat hole you want me to go down and I can't do it. There's no way to win, and plenty of ways to lose."

"And so Harlan Busby hangs."

"And so," Marks replied, "Harlan Busby hangs."

13

Ruff walked slowly back toward the hotel, his eyes combing the dark streets. There was no sign of Fist—if that had been the Indian Ruff saw earlier—only the miners drinking and hell-raising, cutting loose with wild screams, firing their guns in the air while the sheriff laid low and the carpenters continued hammering on the scaffolding for Harlan Busby's hanging.

There were a lot of strangers in town now, drawn from miles around. The hitch rails were crowded with brands unfamiliar and distant.

When Justice entered the hotel dining room, it was crowded to the walls, with some folks standing waiting for tables. He spotted Amy Settle across the room and she waved him over. She was sharing a table with a stranger, a tall, lean man with an indoor look about him but strong square hands sticking out of his tailored coat sleeves. He stood as Ruff came up to the table.

"Hello, Ruff," Amy said. "This is Michael Dorsett."

"Dorsett."

"Heard about you, Mister Justice."

"There wasn't a table to be had. Mister Dorsett invited us to share his."

"What's your line?" Ruff asked, signaling to the waitress, who answered with a weary nod.

"Mister Dorsett is a mine speculator," Amy answered.

"I work for Consolidated out of Denver," Dorsett said. "Now and then I pick up a small claim for them—sometimes I pick up some not so good." He smiled and shrugged. "I've talked to Miss Settle before, though she and her father weren't interested in selling at that time."

"You're here trying to buy it now?"

"Not exactly. I'm here for the horse races, Mister Justice. I've got a blue roan out of a Kentucky dam that'll get out of sight of anything they got around here before you can blink—and that's a fact. Don't lay any money against Blue Boy."

"I never bet on horse races," Ruff said.

"Well, I do. Hobby of mine. It helps when you've got a horse that's never been whipped. This banker here's supposed to have a good gelding—Sagan, is it?—but we'll chew him up and spit him out. That over there is Archie Collins, my jockey." He nodded toward a slight man with his chestnut hair slicked back who was picking at a piece of bread at a nearby table.

"Which is your hobby, Mister Dorsett? Buying mining claims or racing?"

He laughed. "That's what my employer wants to know."

"Are you doing any business with Miss Settle?"

"No." Dorsett shook his head. "Not that I have a poor opinion of her claim, but it's entangled right now and I was sent up here to do a particular job. I've done it, and I don't want to overstep my bounds . . . again." Dorsett laughed and Justice joined in. He liked this lean gambler. He was free-spirited and adventurous. It was a shame Dorsett couldn't see his way clear to offering Amy something for her claim, but encumbered as it was by the bank loan, Ruff could understand the reluctance.

"I've been trying to charm Mister Dorsett into making me an offer, Ruff—all to no avail."

"Well, I wouldn't say that. I'm certainly charmed, Miss Settle, but the boss just doesn't want to pick up any small claims in this area. After we move in, well, maybe that'll be different."

"Move in?"

"Yes. Consolidated is planning on opening up an extensive operation in this area. It'll have to wait until the Indian situation is settled down a little—can't bring equipment across the plains right now—but we're moving in. Moving in big."

"But where?" Amy asked.

"If you turn around and look toward the door, you'll spot a man in a green suit. That man was dead broke this morning and he's working on his first million right now."

The man was Grant Danziger, his flaming red beard combed down over his shirt front, looking a little puzzled and uncertain. He probably hadn't seen that many people together in years.

"That man was sitting on top of the biggest copper strike it's been my good fortune to see," Dorsett said, moving back as the waitress came with a platter of beef and grits for Ruff.

"That's all we got," she said crisply. Then she was gone, harried and exhausted.

Ruff set to eating while Dorsett went on. "Danziger's a wealthy man, friend. Thanks to an alert functionary of ours in Fargo, Amalgamated Mines now owns that claim."

"In Fargo?" Amy said, puzzled.

"They've got someone in the assay office there," Ruff told her, and Dorsett laughed.

"You're an astute man, Mister Justice. Don't repeat

that, please." He talked on, of race horses old and new, of claims that had paid off, of many that had not proved out. They didn't linger long over their meal, with the waiting crowd.

"Come and watch Blue Boy tomorrow," Dorsett said as they went out into the night. "I'll clip this Jack Sagan proper."

"That's what I'd like to do," Amy said as Dorsett strode away picking his teeth. "Trim that crook myself."

"Go on up to your room," Justice said abruptly. "I've just seen someone I have to talk to."

"But, Ruff . . ."

Justice was already on his way across the street. He had seen the man lurking in the shadows, and this time Fist wasn't going to get away without an explanation.

He saw the Mandan turn and walk deeper into the alley, and Justice quickened his pace. He was passing the now-closed general store, turning toward the town smithy, seeing no light but the stars. There, dead in the middle of the narrow alley, crouched down, was Fist.

He rose as Justice came up to him, his eyes sweeping the length of the alley.

"What in hell kind of game is this, Fist? What's the trouble?"

"Not trouble. Or maybe so, but not between us. I do not wish to be seen, Hunter. Now that you have told an entire town about me, there may be some who would wish to kill me."

"You're right there, though it hardly seems they'd bother."

"You have talked to the sheriff?"

"Yes, and it went just about as we'd expected."

"My word is no good."

"Afraid not."

The Mandan was silent. "And what of a white man's word, Hunter?"

"What are you talking about?"

"A white man who also saw the murder of this Blakely. He is here. In this town. Now."

"What man? No one saw it . . . except the man who wrote the letter." The letter that sent Ruff looking for Fist. Of course, how else could the letter-writer have known that Fist saw the murder? He had to have been there himself. Been there and been frightened, not wanting to put himself in the path of Bull Bromfield.

"You're sure?"

"I am sure. I saw this man that day. What he was doing, I do not know. He was, so I think, looking for a place to make another hole in the ground."

"Prospecting?"

"As you say."

"You didn't mention him when you told me the story of what happened."

"Why would I mention this man who was simply watching? He had no part in this," Fist said with peculiar logic.

"But what was needed was a witness. You knew that."

"And there was no witness. He was not here. I did not know, you did not know where he was. What good would it have done to tell you?"

Ruff shook his head at the distance between the mind of Fist and his own. All that Fist had said was perfectly reasonable to the Mandan. He no doubt found Ruff's logic confounding. None of that mattered just now.

"This man is in town?" Ruff asked carefully. "The white man who also saw the murder and who wrote the letter?"

"I do not know," Fist said carefully, "if he wrote a letter." There was a hint of scorn in his tone.

"Where is he?"

"Now? At this place where they sell whiskey, drinking himself stupid."

"Show me."

"Yes," Fist said, "I will do that. How are your wounds, Hunter?"

"Better."

"Good. I think that you will need your strength if you start this confusion. This killer, Bromfield, his friends, will not let you accuse him without danger to you."

"No," Justice answered, "I guess they won't. Come on. I want to see this man."

They walked through the alleys and onto Main Street, where they kept to the shadows. Fist was uneasy. Not frightened, but uncomfortable with the press of men, the sounds of civilization, the popping of fireworks, the drunken hoots.

"This is the place," the Mandan said as they reached a saloon called Trail's End.

"Let's have a look."

They stepped into the alley and peered in through a greasy side window, seeing nothing but blurs and moving silhouettes. The piano within was very loud, very out of tune.

"I can see nothing," Fist said.

"All right. Come on."

"I cannot go into this place where they have whiskey."

"You'll go in all right—not by the front door, though. I want to find this man, Fist. I have to."

"Yes." Fist sighed with resignation.

They walked together down the alley to the back of the saloon where empty barrels were stacked three high. Ruff tried the door and they went in, through a storeroom, the piano, the sounds of laughter growing louder.

Ruff cracked an inner door open, and a blaze of light met his eyes. He could see half of the saloon, see a bearded miner tramping past with a painted, red-gowned girl at arm's length, dancing clumsily. He could see three different poker games, see the intent eyes watching the flickering spin of a roulette wheel, see the serious drinkers at the bar.

"Look in there, then," Ruff said, and Fist, his nose wrinkled with disgust, looked through the crack.

"Yes."

"You see him?" Ruff asked eagerly.

"Yes." Fist shrugged.

"Point him out to me."

"You see there the man in the red shirt. It is not him, but the next one over, the smaller man."

Ruff saw him, all right. About twenty, blond, blue-eyed, looking shy, somber, and quite drunk.

"You're sure?"

"Ai! Please, Hunter, the music hurts my head. Yes, I am sure. Let me go to the mountains now. I must have been mad to come here."

"Not mad, but a good friend, Fist."

"Yes. A stupid good friend. Let us leave now. Please!"

They went out through the storeroom into the alley, where Fist stood taking deep cleansing breaths. "Now I will go. Do not try to stop me, Hunter. I have involved myself in your white troubles, but no more. I have been a little mad; your spirits are strong. I have helped you, now release me from this obligation."

Fist was deadly serious and Ruff rested a hand on his shoulder, telling him, "I release you. You have done all any man can do. I am grateful."

"Yes. Then, I will go. To the bald mountain, Hunter.

There an old man can find peace, and it is peace that I desire now."

He started away, stopped, and said without turning back, "I wish you luck too, Hunter. One day we will hunt together and I will tell you the old stories."

"That would be fine, Fist. I hope it will be so."

Then he was gone, a shadow merging with the darkness. Ruff stood looking after him for a time, then turned sharply and started toward the Trail's End's front door.

Ruff took a look in over the batwing doors, seeing the dense smoke, the even thicker mob of miners. It was no good going in there now, he decided, and he crossed the street to sit in the shadows of the general store's awning, watching as the night passed by.

The carpenters had quit on the scaffolding, the streets were less crowded now, though those men that passed were a hell of a lot drunker.

It was nearly midnight when the young man with the blond hair came staggering out of the Trail's End and started walking unsteadily up the street. He never noticed the long shadow of the man who fell in behind him, following him toward the stable at the end of the rutted alley called First Avenue.

"Talk to you?"

The young man halted and turned around. He was beneath the huge old sycamore, the tall man before him deep in shadow. "What do you want?"

"Just stand where you are."

"What is this?" He turned as if he would run and heard the heavy metallic clicking of a hammer being drawn back.

"Stand steady," Ruff Justice repeated.

"What the hell is this? I haven't got any money on me. A little change, maybe. Who are you?"

"I just want to have a little talk."

"About what?" he asked, his voice trembling.

"A man named Blakely."

"Oh, Jesus!" the kid cried. "Bull Bromfield sent you."

"No."

"Listen, I haven't got any money with me, but I can get some. Sure. A few hundred dollars anyway. Five hundred. You can take that and tell Bull you got me! I'll leave this country and never come back. I swear to you, I'll . . ."

"Shut up. Let's step out of the road, shall we?"

They went deeper into the shadows. There had once been a prospect hole right down in town here, and when the vein went bad, they had moved on, leaving the office and supply sheds. It was to these that Ruff took the kid.

"Stand right there," Ruff told him, looking back toward the road to see that they hadn't been followed. "Listen, Bull Bromfield didn't send me. No one sent me. I'm here because there's a man in jail who's going to be hung tomorrow and you can stop it. And you will."

"They'll kill me!" The kid's face was white, agonized in the starlight.

"Yes, and if you don't tell what you know, I'll have you. What's your name?"

"George Hall," he muttered, his head hanging.

"You wrote that letter to the sheriff?"

"Yes."

"From here?"

The kid sighed. "I gave it to a friend who was going to Bismarck. He mailed it back here. I didn't want any trouble."

"But it's all right if Harlan Busby hangs."

"I did the best I could do!"

"All right. Forget all of that." Ruff hunkered down against the grass, holding his pistol loosely as he looked up at Hall. "You've got to come forward now. There's no time left and the Indian's word is just no good."

"Yes. Yes, dammit, I know that. I tried getting drunk to . . . Well, I can't let him hang. But dammit all, I'm scared!"

"Yeah. I know it," Ruff said, and it wasn't unkindly. The kid had the right to be scared. What he didn't have was the right to stand by and see a man hung. "You saw Bull Bromfield do the job?"

The answer was barely audible. "Yes."

"With that club he carries?"

"Yes."

"All right." Ruff stood up. "You ready to find the sheriff and tell him?"

"Not hardly." The kid cracked a weak smile. "But you're going to see that I do it anyway, aren't you?"

"Afraid so."

"All right." He pulled himself together. He had sobered up almighty fast when the excitement started. "Let's do it. But damn you for making me go in!"

They walked slowly, carefully, back toward the sheriff's office, Ruff hoping that Marks was in. He didn't think the lawman would want him sneaking into his room again this time of night.

They were in luck—Marks was there. Justice banged open the door and they discovered the sheriff behind his desk, pouring a stiff drink of whiskey, his face red and swollen, his eyes pouched.

"What is it?" Marks grunted.

"A man here wants to talk to you," Justice said, closing the door behind them. He leaned against the cell doors, arms folded, watching as George Hall hesitantly spilled his story, which was essentially the same as Fist's. Marks turned morose, drinking his whiskey, pouring another one. He muttered under his breath the entire time, seeing his job, his pension slip out from under him.

"You're sure, damn you, Hall!"

"I couldn't mistake Bull Bromfield for another living man," the kid said miserably.

"Yeah. What in hell do I do now?" the sheriff said.

"Now," Justice spoke up, "you arrest Bull Bromfield."

"Yeah." Marks drained his glass and smiled wryly. "I guess I do."

"Want me to come along?"

"You? Hell, no! Nothing would be surer to fire Bull off. I don't want this to come to shooting." Slyly the sheriff observed, "If it's just me, he may laugh at me, give me hell, but he won't take it seriously. He'll count on being sprung in an hour or so."

"You're probably right. I'd hate to see him make a run, though."

"You're out of this, Justice. Tell you what, you can find Hawkes for me—he's at the Whiskey Well playing faro. I'd like him around, such as he is. And he can watch Hall here too."

"Me! Look, Marks . . ."

"Shut up. You're going into the lockup. You're all the evidence I've got and I'm not going to go halfway with this. If you get gone, I'm left up the creek. No, I'm keeping an eye on you, Mister Hall."

Hall started to argue again, then just gave it up—maybe he realized this was the only place in town where he would be safe once this got out.

"What about . . . ?" Ruff inclined his head toward the cell where Harlan Busby slept or lay awake listening hopefully or desperately.

"Bring Hawkes over for me," the sheriff said, his mouth dry, "and I'll let you have him. He's a witness, too, though he doesn't have much to tell. I want him to stay in town, preferably under guard."

"All right." Marks had gotten his keys out and Ruff opened the door. "Sheriff, I'm gaining a new respect for you. Don't lose your nerve."

"My nerve!" Marks laughed. "No, not that. I'm running the chance of losing my ass complete, but I'll see this through."

Ruff found Hawkes losing at a faro table and he managed to drag him out without too much trouble. He refused to tell the deputy what it was about, leaving that to Marks.

When they entered the sheriff's office, Harlan Busby was out of his cell, a shell of a man, crumpled and pale, his eyes feverish, hopeful, and frightened.

"What the hell?" Hawkes asked.

"Busby's cleared. There's a witness in there. You watch him. I'm going after Bull Bromfield." Marks rattled it all off conversationally as he got his hat and gun belt. Hawkes, dazed, only nodded. "And stay here, Hawkes! Don't go running after Jack Sagan." The sheriff leveled a warning finger at his deputy. Hawkes babbled something and turned a little red.

The sheriff looked at Ruff and shook his head. "Mister, I wish to hell you'd of stayed wherever in hell you were, because you've sure brought me a situation. You surely have."

Then he was gone, out into the night, leaving the door open. Ruff stepped forward to look down at Harlan Busby. "You ready, Mister Busby?"

"Pardon me? Are we leaving?"

"We're leaving. You're free."

"Well, then . . ." He rose, looked toward the cell, at the deputy, and then nodded. "Let's be going."

The streets were still busy. Harlan Busby looked around him with astonishment. Life outside that cell was still unreal to him. Ruff took him up the back way to the hotel, climbed the stairs, and walked to the second-floor room. He tapped on the door and after a minute the gray-haired woman in her colorless wrapper opened it.

"Harlan!" Emily Busby fell back in astonishment,

her hands going to her mouth as her eyes flooded with tears. Harlan Busby took a step forward and she flung herself into his arms, sobbing softly as the door closed, shutting the scene away from Ruff Justice.

Outside, men still whooped in celebration. The firecrackers still popped and crackled. It was noisy, but it was nothing compared to what was going to happen now. The next explosion was going to be the big one. Ruff had hunted far and wide for the fuse to the powder keg this town was sitting on. Now he had found it and calmly lit the fuse. Tomorrow was the Fourth and there was going to be a display of fireworks like nothing Bear Fork had ever seen.

14

The morning streets were ugly. There was an ominous undercurrent Ruff could sense as soon as he went out. The miners, still drunk, sullen, stood together in knots on the street corners, deliberately not looking toward the jail, where their boss was being held.

The sun was just rising, but it was already hot in Bear Fork, promising to grow hotter.

Justice ate a leisurely breakfast, conscious of the angry eyes that watched him; then he walked the length of the street to the sheriff's office.

Trying the door, he found it locked. He rapped loudly and it was a while before a cautious answering voice responded.

"Who is it?" Hawkes asked.

"Me. Ruff Justice."

"You get on away. The sheriff doesn't want you around."

"Open up, Hawkes."

There was another long pause, then the sound of the heavy bar being slid back, the creaking of the hinges as the door swung open.

Hawkes, cradling a scattergun in his arms, stood nervously before Justice. "What do you want, scout?"

"Just wanted to see if the sheriff had any instructions for Busby, for me." Ruff took a seat without being invited. "Also thought someone might have found my horse."

"Your horse?"

"Little roan quarter horse. I lost him up to the bald mountain and I'm afoot, not liking it."

"Haven't heard a word."

"Who is that?"

The voice crackled across the room, a booming accusation, rife with hatred. Bull Bromfield was suddenly there, pressed against the bars of the cell. Hawkes took an involuntary step backward as the mine boss shouted again, "Who the hell is out there! Justice? You son of a bitch, Ruff Justice, you'll be dead before this day is over."

"Maybe. There's that chance every morning, isn't there?" Ruff walked nearer to the cell. "But I'd be willing to bet I'll live long enough to see you hang."

A big hand shot through the bars, coming inches short of Ruff's shirt front. Bromfield's eyes bulged, the veins in his throat throbbed.

"Sorry you'll miss the sack race today," Ruff said. Then he nodded and went out, Bromfield's curses filling the air. Justice stood before the sheriff's office, smiling softly for a minute. The sun was hot, the street dusty. The miners never seemed to move as they glared across at him.

The sound of hoofbeats brought Ruff's head around. The sorrel gelding pulled up sharply, lifting a fine cloud of dust. Aboard the sorrel was Jack Sagan in a gray suit and white hat, his lean face furious. The sheriff was with him, reluctantly swinging down, looking up the street and down, avoiding Ruff's eyes.

" 'Morning, Sheriff," Ruff said, and then he turned his attention to Sagan.

"You bloody bastard," Sagan sputtered, "what the hell are you up to?"

"Me?" Ruff shrugged, his face innocent. "Just watching the workings of the law. I'll be watching it when Bromfield swings. And maybe, if he decides at the last minute to tell us who sent him out to kill Blakely and Sam Settle, I'll be watching the workings of the law as they pop that trap on you, Mister Sagan."

"He'll never hang, I promise you that. You see those men. You're taking their jobs from them. They'll tear this jail to kindling and then we'll see who swings, Mister Justice!"

"Could be." Ruff was looking at the lathered gelding Sagan rode. "Think this animal can take Michael Dorsett's Blue Boy?"

Sagan's mouth opened but no sound came out of it. He stormed up the plankwalk to stand before the office door waiting for the sheriff, who followed miserably, casting a last dolorous glance in Ruff Justice's direction.

Justice smiled in return and started back up the street. Yes, they were watching him. To the miners' minds this was the man who had gotten their boss locked up for murder. They might have feared and hated Bull Bromfield and his club, but they hated the man who had taken him still more. They knew, every one of them, that the northern lodes were drying up, that Amalgamated was dying. They knew now that Danziger had sold out, that Busby had his mine back, that the work around Bear Fork was going to wither and die. Their anger was based on unreasoning loyalty and fear, but it was a real and deep anger.

Justice did his best to ignore it. He found Amy Settle in the hotel dining room with Michael Dorsett, and he was in time to witness the astonishing conversation that followed.

"Hello, Ruff," Amy said, and there was a pleasing light in her eyes.

Ruff smiled in return, nodded to Dorsett, and sat

down. "Just saw Sagan's gelding. He's ridden it to a frazzle this morning. I suppose your Blue Boy will win in a walk now."

"Yes?" Dorsett looked disturbed by the news. "Too bad. I like a good race. Doesn't mean much if the other man's rider gets bumped off or the horse pulls up lame. I wonder if he'll withdraw?"

"Not if there's money involved," Amy guessed.

"Oh, there's money involved all right. A thousand-dollar wager." Dorsett winked meaningfully.

"A thousand!" Amy's eyes caught fire.

"Quite a bit, isn't it? Well, I've won more and lost more. I'm hooked on gambling, maybe. But as I say, with Blue Boy I'm going to win a hell of a lot more than I lose. If I ever do lose with him—hasn't been whipped yet."

"I could beat him," Amy said.

Dorsett smiled, wondering if he had heard right. "Pardon me?"

"I say I've got a horse that could beat him."

"Oh, have you?" Dorsett laughed.

"Yes, I have," Amy said, leaning forward intently. "For a thousand dollars."

"Have you got a thousand dollars, Miss Settle? Sorry, but even if you were serious, we couldn't do any business there."

"But I *am* serious. And I haven't got a thousand dollars, but I've got my father's claim. There's money owing on it, as you know, but it's even less than a thousand now. Don't you see what I'm offering you? I'll race you for a thousand dollars. If I should lose, I'll sign over the claim; then all you would have to do is pay the bank what's owing on the loan—and it would be a cheap price for that claim. You've seen it, you know what it's worth, what it will be worth when your Consolidated company comes in."

"I'm sorry," Dorsett said. "I can see you're serious.

But it wouldn't be fair. Honestly. You haven't got anything that can touch Blue Boy, and we both know it. I would be stealing your mine."

"No! You wouldn't be. Tell him, Ruff!"

"Her horse might be able to beat you. I'd lay money it could," Justice put in.

"You can't mean it." Dorsett smiled again, more uncertainly. "My cash against title to your mine, but I pay the bank if I win."

"Yes."

"But you'd have nothing at all in the world if you lost, Miss Settle. I really couldn't . . ."

"I'll have nothing anyway by tomorrow when that note comes due, don't you see? You're the only chance I've got."

"I just don't know. It doesn't seem right."

Justice spoke up again. "Amy lays out the course and I'll ride."

"I'll ride myself, Mister Justice. Yes, let me lay out the course and I'll beat Blue Boy."

Dorsett was both puzzled and amused. He seriously did not want to take the woman's mine in an unfair contest, but both Amy and Justice seemed to think the contest would be equal. That stirred his wagering blood, his horseman's pride.

"Whatever you say," he answered finally. "I don't feel right about it, but you seem so anxious . . . Yes, I'll run you for a thousand against your title to the Settle mine."

"On a handshake?" Amy asked, sticking out her small, lovely hand.

Dorsett grinned and solemnly took it. "Your word is good enough if mine is, Miss Settle."

"Fine. Do you want to see the other horse?"

"No, it's not necessary. Explain the course to me and my jockey, and we'll have at it whenever you choose."

"Right now." Amy rose, tossing her napkin down, her face flushed with excitement. Ruff sat with his chin on his palm, watching expressionlessly. The waitress had just arrived to take Ruff's order, but Amy waved her away impatiently. "Are you up to it?"

Dorsett laughed again. "You're the most impulsive thing I've ever met, Miss Settle, but, yes, I'm up to it if you are."

"We'll be out front in ten minutes," she said excitedly. "Are you coming, Ruff? Please hurry."

"She doesn't want to give me time to change my mind," Dorsett said.

"You're exactly right, my friend. She'll want cash. Have you got it with you?"

Dorsett smiled, but the expression slowly faded to an uneasy curiosity. "I've got it," he said a little more soberly.

Ruff nodded and went out, following Amy, who was pushing her way through the breakfast crowd toward the front door of the hotel.

Dorsett's smile came back with a rush when he saw the competition for that morning: the long-legged, loose-jointed hammerhead chestnut with the beginnings of a swayed back.

"Is this a joke?" He looked to Ruff Justice. "Look, my friend, I'm not a man to take advantage. I know the girl is desperate, but . . ." A hand waved derisively toward the horse finished the sentence.

"I'll promise you a good race if you let the lady have her way," Ruff answered, and there was no humor to be seen in his eyes. "To tell you the truth, she's fixin' to take advantage of *you*. Go through with it. At your own risk."

Dorsett looked to the skies, his arms spread. "They're all mad in Bear Fork."

A few miners had started to gather around, listening to find out what was happening. Their heads turned in unison at the sound of hoofbeats on the nearly empty street. It was Dorsett's jockey on Blue Boy, a strapping deep-chested, short-coupled blue roan with fire in his eyes, strength and explosive vitality in those tapering legs. The roan sidestepped down Main Street, tossing its head so that its nearly white mane swirled around its neck like a miniature snowstorm.

"This ain't no race," one of the miners said. "It's a massacree!"

The long runner managed to stretch out its long neck and bite him on the haunch, and the miner leaped away, cursing violently before stalking away to look for a glass of whiskey to start the day.

"Ready?" Amy Settle had dashed back to her room to change into jeans and cotton shirt. Now she stood pert and lively before Michael Dorsett, her lips pursed seriously.

"Yes," Dorsett answered, glancing at the long runner, "if you are." He turned and gestured to his jockey. "Archie, come on over here and we'll lay out the course."

The tiny man in silks of silver and blue, whip tucked under his arm, came to stand beside his boss.

"This is a match race for a thousand-dollar purse," Dorsett announced to the crowd. "Blue Boy against . . ."

"He's got no name," Amy said.

"Against this chestnut horse owned by Miss Amy Settle. Now, Miss Settle, if you'll tell us how we're to run—down the street? Up and back? Around the town?"

"To my claim and back," she said.

"That's nearly fifteen miles!"

"Yes, sir, it is," Amy agreed.

Dorsett rubbed his chin speculatively. He looked at Blue Boy, all fire and lean muscle, and then at the long runner. "Well, I certainly wouldn't choose that kind of distance, but I told you to name your course. I can't believe Blue Boy will lose at any distance. All right, young lady, it's on."

They explained it to Archie, telling him which road to take. "Just go south and keep going. There's a purple rose bush in front of my house and it's in bloom. The only roses around for miles. First one there plucks a rose and brings it back as proof he's run the distance."

The cinches were tightened, Archie given a leg-up into the light racing saddle. Ruff gave Amy a hug and a smile. "Luck to you, lady. I'll see you when you get back."

The streets were fuller now and people cleared out of the way to stand watching. Ruff said to Dorsett, "My friend, you've been suckered. Better start counting that gold."

"The moment I see the lady coming down the street with a purple rose," he said. Dorsett knew something had happened now, but he didn't seem worried about it, more amused, and Ruff had the idea the man could afford to lose the thousand if it came to that.

"Start 'em, Mister Dorsett?"

"Sure."

The horses were turned, and as Dorsett lifted his hat, both riders shortened rein and tensed. Blue Boy was ready, stamping at the ground, going sideways, up on hind legs while the chestnut looked ready to doze off.

"Go!" Dorsett dropped his hat and they were off. Blue Boy was to top speed in three flying bounds and there was a cheer of appreciation as it stretched out its neck and dashed the length of the street to take the south road. The chestnut moved forward at a steady lope, Amy whipping it with her hat, trying to generate speed.

Dorsett laughed with embarrassment and apologized.

"Sorry—the poor girl, I almost feel sorry enough for her to give her the thousand."

"Think about that after we've seen the result," Justice said. Then he stepped up onto the hotel's plankwalk, to rest in the shade of the awning, noticing that the chestnut had nearly reached the end of the street. "You ever read fables, Mister Dorsett?"

"Fables?"

"Never mind. I had a particular one in mind right now. Yes, sir. I'd start counting that money, were I you."

Amy swung onto the south road seeing nothing of Blue Boy but his dust. The chestnut was warmed to its task now and it ran fluidly, loping at that peculiar pace it had chosen for its own. The whipping did no good, the shouting, and so she settled in, hunched forward anxiously, hoping and praying as the long runner moved toward home.

The road rose and then wound down through the hills, and as she reached the crest, Amy could see Blue Boy and Archie far below, perhaps two miles ahead. They appeared like a miniature horse and man, sending up a miniature cloud of dust as the blue roan glided down the hill road.

"Why in hell don't you run like that? Can't you see how a horse is *supposed* to move?"

The long runner behaved as he always had. He ran tirelessly, showing no bursts of speed, no sign of weariness. Panic began to set in. Amy was damp with perspiration. The sun was hot and white in a clear sky, the dust stifling.

She was two miles from her house when she saw the approaching dark form, a dark form that lightened and then took on form. It was a blur of color, a magnificent blend of strength and beauty. Blue Boy, and on his back perched Archie, holding high a single purple rose. The roan flew past them, not ruffling the chestnut a bit, and Amy, seeing all of her possessions slip away, began to thump on the chestnut's head with her fist. It might as well have been a feather, a swarm of light-footed gnats. The long runner paid no attention whatsoever.

Her heart was racing wildly when she finally spotted her familiar house. It seemed hours, endless agonizing hours, before the long runner reached the front door stoop across the valley and Amy swung down on the run to tear a rose from the bush, slashing her hand on thorns.

She was aboard again, digging her heels into the chestnut's flanks, and again it started, slowly, to gain momentum. The long runner reached its usual speed and settled in, and Amy felt tears stinging her eyes as they returned to the road so far behind Blue Boy that there was not even the scent of his dust in the air.

Up the long grade her eyes scoured the road ahead, searching for that roan horse. Nothing. He was up and over already! On the downslope toward town. "Please," she begged the chestnut, leaning low toward its ears, "please, hurry."

She might as well have told the mountains to move. The chestnut ran on, up that long, winding grade never slackening its pace, never seeming to extend itself. Then they crested and the jumbled, dark form of Bear Fork lay beneath them.

The road, familiar and broad, lay through the deep ranks of pines. It was with a sense of helpless panic that Amy rode on, the town growing larger, the trees closing in around her, the rose crushed in her hand, the thorns biting her palm.

Then suddenly she saw it: the blue roan running at an uneven pace toward the town; Archie, in his silver and blue silks, standing in the high stirrups whipping the exhausted animal's flanks for all he was worth.

The roan was lathered, worn out. Archie looked

across his shoulder and Amy could see his upper lip curl back, see the indignant shock on his face.

"Come on! Please," she said to the chestnut, but the long runner was deaf to all pleas and urgings. He simply ran as he himself had chosen.

Amy could see the buildings of the town again now as the trees parted. They were near enough so that she could read the signs painted on the buildings. The roan was six lengths in front of her; Archie, going to the whip insistently, was up in the stirrups, far forward, and he turned onto Main Street first, a roar coming from the throats of the Fourth of July Main Street crowd.

"Please!" Amy said, and she found that she couldn't even see the finish line for the tears.

She saw a blur of gray to her right and realized with sudden exultance that it was the flank of the roan, that she was within three-quarters of a length of Blue Boy's nose. She beat furiously at the chestnut and suddenly, incredibly, the long runner found another pace, one he had perhaps been searching for all of his days. He surged forward, moving at a hard run, ungainly legs flying, and Amy Settle crossed the finish line, the purple rose held high as the crowd cheered and cursed, threw down hats or sailed them high into the sky.

When she had reached the end of the street, dazed and exultant at once, she turned and returned, seeing the tall man in black jeans and maroon shirt detach himself from the crowd to come forward and stretch out his arms, swinging her from the saddle to hold her tightly.

"You did good, woman," Ruff Justice said, kissing her as she laughed and cried at once. The chestnut horse tried to bite his leg and he had to slap its head away. Upstreet a chain of firecrackers was exploded and the brass band began to play. Together, leading the long runner, Ruff and Amy walked toward Michael Dorsett, who stood shaking his head, soberly weighing the little canvas sack he held that contained fifty gold double eagles.

"You did it," he said, trying to smile. "Showed me up proper."

"Don't you believe it," Amy said. "That horse of yours will never be beaten under ten miles. You have my word for it."

"No?" Dorsett brightened a little. "Walk him, Archie. Don't sulk. Cool that horse down properly." He handed the gold sack to Amy and then offered, "May I buy you a drink?"

There wasn't time for an answer. From uptown the gunshots began. Someone had decided that the Fourth was as good a time as any for a war.

"They got the sheriff," someone screamed with malicious pleasure, and Ruff started at a run toward the jailhouse, Amy's screams, the popping of fireworks, the louder barking of the guns filling his ears.

He took it all in at once: Jack Sagan sitting his sorrel, around him a mob of miners waving fists and clubs. The eight men with the heavy timber banging it against the front door of the sheriff's office, the pale-blue haze of settling gunsmoke, and the face of Bull Bromfield at the outer cell window, twisted and reddened by rage as he thrust out a vengeful finger and screamed.

"There he is! It's Ruff Justice. Kill him! Kill him!"

15

At the sound of Bull Bromfield's voice the mob wheeled and started toward Justice, all of them but the men with the battering ram, who continued trying to smash through the jailhouse door. Ruff drew his Colt and put three rounds at the feet of the advancing mob, and they halted, backing up a little, pressing against each other, snarling and growling.

"Get him, damn you," Bromfield screamed. "What's stopping you?"

"Justice!" The voice was that of Hawkes, who was locked inside the jail with Sheriff Marks. "Help us! Get some men!"

There was stark panic in Hawkes' voice. Ruff kept his eyes on the mob, which was straining at the tether, needing just the right word to send them surging forward in a human wave that would tear Justice apart.

Get more men? Where? This was a mining town, and it was the company against the law. Justice didn't expect much help.

"You boys are asking for trouble," he told the miners in a quiet voice. "First thing you know you'll have killed the sheriff."

"Or you, you bastard!"

"Or me," Ruff acknowledged with a smile. "And

then you've got nowhere to go. The federal marshals will move in looking for you, every one of you. Maybe the army as well."

"It'd be worth it."

"Would it? What in hell are you fighting for? For Bromfield, who's a sadistic killer—yes, it's God's own truth that he clubbed two men to death—or for Sagan, who only wants to line his own pockets?"

"We stand by the company."

"The company's dead! You may as well know that. Look to Sagan, to Bull Bromfield. Why are they fighting like this? Because the Amalgamated claims are dried up. You're the people that should know that best. You're the ones that work in those shafts. Seen much high-grade stuff lately? Or are the veins shriveling up? You know what's happening up there."

"There's new holes coming in."

"Yeah? Down south?" Ruff took a few steps forward. Ignoring Sagan and the ranting Bromfield, he addressed himself to a big blond-bearded miner who seemed to be the mob leader.

"That's right—the Danziger claim . . ."

"Danziger sold out this morning to Consolidated," Ruff said, and he was surprised to hear a confirming voice at his shoulder.

"That's right, I did," Grant Danziger, splendid in his new green suit, carrying a shotgun, told them. "To Mister Dorsett here."

And Dorsett was there, sitting Blue Boy, holding a Winchester repeater. "You men will likely have a job with us," Dorsett told them, "but we'll have no wanted men, no murderers."

"Kill them," Bromfield shouted, his voice cracking with the unalloyed rage in him.

"Ruff?"

Justice glanced to his left, saw the rifle tossed neatly to him by Amy Settle, and he nodded, holstering his

Colt to hold the big Spencer buffalo gun casually in his hands. Amy herself had a rifle. It looked huge in her hands, but the woman knew what it was for.

"My claim's not going over to Amalgamated either, boys," Amy Settle told them. "Mister Sagan? I've got a thousand dollars here. I'm paying off the note."

"That leaves only the Busby-Blakely, doesn't it?" Ruff asked. "Except that, thanks to a man with some guts, Harlan Busby is free again to run his own mine. Thanks to a man who came forward and told the truth: that Bromfield killed Blakely to jump that claim. That man's inside the jail now. How long do you think he'll last once Bromfield is free?"

"What are you waiting for?" Sagan shrieked, his voice high and wavering, but the logic of the situation was getting through to the mob.

"You boys have already wounded the sheriff. Any more of this and, by God, they'll have a use for that gallows, won't they?"

"Why are you standing there listening to all of this?" Sagan screamed.

"Yeah, and why aren't you down front here where the shooting's going to be?" the blond miner asked. "Maybe," he said to the men in back of him, "we are fools. What are we fighting for? Maybe I'll be out of a job tonight, but I'll enjoy the Fourth of July a hell of a lot more above the ground. I never did like you, Sagan. And Bromfield—Well, I've seen him thump the boys with that club of his. Yeah, he'd do murder, all right. Probably did. You men do what you want; me, I'm going to have me some whiskey and dance with a woman at the Whiskey Well. It beats having my guts opened up by that buffalo gun Justice is carrying."

The man tipped his hat to Amy, turned, and stalked off, followed by a few of the others. Sagan's curses followed them all the way down the street.

Ruff still hadn't moved. It was a stalemate: the

miners, in the face of the guns, were hesitant about going forward; Justice had some grave doubts about the wisdom of trying to press through the crowd of miners to where Jack Sagan sat his horse.

It was then that the jailhouse door was punctured by three bullets, all aimed high, sending showers of splinters into the crowd. The men with the battering ram took to their heels and a moment later the door opened.

Sheriff Marks stood there, blood streaming down his face, staining his white shirt. He had to lean against the door to hold himself up, and he was mad, fighting mad.

"You all get the hell out of here or I start shooting. Justice, you and those other people are deputized, and I'm ordering you to shoot any man who's still standing here thirty seconds from now."

"All right," Justice answered coldly, drawing back the hammer on that terrifying .56 repeater he carried. Amy, Grant Danziger, and Michael Dorsett all cocked their weapons, the sound inordinately loud suddenly as the miners fell silent, backing away.

"You, Jack Sagan," Marks shouted, "you're under arrest for conspiracy to murder . . . for inciting a riot . . . hell, I don't know what all, but you're under arrest!"

Sagan wasn't ready to be arrested. Before anyone could react, he had drawn a Smith & Wesson pistol and fired two rounds at the sheriff, who hit the deck to avoid being hit. Then Sagan slapped the spurs to that sorrel of his, trampling several men in front of him as he rode hell for it up Main Street.

Justice spun, saw Blue Boy standing beside Dorsett, and leaped into the saddle, kneeing the roan to get it started.

Sagan's horse was quick, but it wasn't even close to matching Blue Boy. That morning's race might have taken some of the steam out of the blue roan, but it had plenty of speed left.

Sagan made it out of town and was heading into the oaks growing along the creek when Justice caught him. He kicked out of the stirrups and jumped, grabbing Sagan by the coat collar, and they went down beneath the feet of the horses, rolling down the grassy embankment beside the creek.

Justice felt pain tear through his wounded chest, and as they landed, the breath was jolted from him, but he was alert enough to see Sagan come to his feet, start to bring up that Smith & Wesson of his, to see the fire in the banker's eyes, the hate that twisted his mouth into an animal snarl.

Justice drew and fired, hearing Sagan's bullet whip past his head to plow into one of the big oaks. Ruff's bullets didn't miss.

He fired three times, the first two from his knees. Sagan was hurled back, his mouth spilling blood, two neat smoldering holes in his vest front.

"Damn you . . ." Sagan managed to say, and he tried to bring the pistol up again as Justice walked toward him, Colt at waist level. "I'll kill . . ." the banker gurgled, and Justice shot him again.

"No," Justice said to the dying man, "I guess you've done all the killing you're going to."

Sagan's eyes were still fixed on Ruff. His fingers clenched and unclenched, trying to pull the trigger to a gun that wasn't there any longer. The eyes were savage, dark, mad—and then they weren't anything but two still, colorless orbs staring up at the July sky through the canopy of oak boughs.

Justice heard the approaching horses and he looked upslope to see Amy leap from the long runner's back and charge down the hill to throw herself into his arms. He held her while she sobbed and cussed him, kissed him and laughed hysterically.

Finally calming herself, she looked at the body of Jack Sagan and said, "Let's go, Ruff. I didn't care for his company when he was alive, I don't want to put up with it now."

The streets were oddly quiet when they reached Bear Fork again. There was a small crowd gathered in front of the brass band's platform, knots of men in front of the saloons, a few strolling couples dressed in their holiday best, but outside of that, it was a quiet Fourth.

"We had our fireworks early," Dorsett commented.

"Yes, I guess we did."

The doctor was working over Sheriff Marks, who was out of sorts more than anything else and kept shouting for whiskey. Sagan had missed him with both shots he had fired at the sheriff, and the only real wound he suffered was the split scalp he had gotten when the miners had jumped him earlier.

"When's the trial?" Ruff asked him.

"As soon as I can get it," Marks spat back. "I don't want that bastard sitting around here any longer than necessary. Hawkes! Where's that damn whiskey?"

Ruff looked in on George Hall, who appeared composed, content in his jail cell now that the trouble was over. "They had me sweating it for a while, though," he admitted. "You were right about one thing—Bromfield told me—if they'd stormed this jail, I would have been murdered."

"Well, you don't have to worry about that now. Sit back and relax. You won't be in here long."

Amy was outside waiting, hands behind her back, eyes looking almost with fondness up Main Street. She turned with a smile when Ruff came out.

"How's it feel to be young, free, and rich?" Justice asked.

"Fine! Just fine. I don't know about that 'rich,' though."

"I think you've got a very good chance of becoming rich. Dorsett thinks so, too, and he should know."

"Maybe . . ." She looked away momentarily. "Would you like to share it with me? I mean," she went on hastily, "just for a while."

"I've got to get back, Amy," Justice said, and again she turned her eyes away.

"An important job, is that it?" she asked, and her voice fluttered a little.

"I don't know about that, but it's a life I like. Damned if I know why, but I do."

"When?"

"Tonight, I expect."

She shrugged. "Well, then, we've got today."

"All of it."

"Have you ever been in a sack race? Pa and I tried last year, but we didn't even finish. Look at those legs on you," she said, putting her hands on his waist, smiling, although her eyes were cloudy. "Shall we have a try at it?"

"We'll try it all, Amy. We'll dance and listen to the band and watch the fireworks. It'll be a fine Fourth," he promised.

It was, and when it was nearly over, they sat on the hill rise near the river watching the spray of crimson and blue rockets against a starry sky, lying there in each other's arms as the Fourth exhausted itself in a last merry spasm before the long parade of workdays returned.

Ruff had been given Jack Sagan's sorrel horse. It didn't seem to be so much gratitude as a desire to get rid of everything, everyone that could remind Bear Fork of its violent soul.

He waited in the darkness, a strange and moody darkness that followed the explosive evening of star showers and bursting pinwheels, but Amy didn't return. She was a wise woman—good-byes can only be stretched so far.

He swung aboard and there was no one there to say good-bye. The town, enervated, shamed, spent, slept on, and there was hardly a light across the valley.

Ruff turned the sorrel eastward and headed home.

16

There were no birds singing as Ruff Justice rode down the pine-clad slopes toward Johnstown the following morning. There was a heaviness to the orange-gold dawn air that he didn't understand until he saw the town lying cold and silent.

It wasn't a town any longer. The bandit had had his due.

John Schick had been no prophet—the Indians had returned and they had destroyed his larcenous operation. The stone buildings were scorched and blackened by flame. The store was nothing but a heap of ash. The trees surrounding the place might have been formed of wrought iron. They were stark and bare and without foliage.

The hooves of Jack Sagan's sorrel kicked up black dust and ash, and the animal stepped lightly enough to let Ruff know that the ashes were still hot.

He swung down with his rifle and walked to the stone house, kicking open the charred door. There was no one inside, no one without. All of his goods had been taken.

Ruff swung aboard again and sat for a minute staring at the ruins of Johnstown; then, tugging down his hat, he rode out onto the clean and limitless plains, a swift horse beneath him, a sweet memory of a golden-haired girl riding with him.

He rode warily, knowing the Sioux were close around, but he saw no Indian sign that morning, none into the afternoon. He decided they were probably sleeping off John Schick's whiskey somewhere.

There was nothing but the long-grass plains, the empty blue sky, the meadowlarks his horse kicked from the grass, the white, wind-drifted fields of black-eyed Susans.

He slept well that night and awoke refreshed, relaxed. Two days would put him into Fort Lincoln.

A few clouds had drifted in—high, white, puffy. Their shadows raced Ruff Justice across the land. He spotted a large buffalo herd that morning and veered far to the north, avoiding them and any possible Indian hunters.

The breeze was light, the sky blue, the horse fresh. Ruff threw back his head and began to sing.

I was just a young man in the spring of fifty-fo'
Down upon my luck, I did agree to go
And spend a pleasant summer on the trail of the buffalo . . .

It seemed then that a wasp stung him on the shoulder and he swatted at it in annoyance. The wasp had stung him and it was burning terribly. There was a distant roaring in his ears, like faraway thunder, and with shocked confusion he realized that he was tumbling from his horse, that the fire of the wasp's sting had become fierce, boring pain.

"I'm damned if I'm not shot," he thought in amazement as he hit the ground, seeing the sorrel kick up its hind feet and dance away across the long grass.

Ruff lay on his back, blinking at the brilliant sky for long minutes before it all became starkly clear and his heart began to hammer, screaming for his attention. The instinct for survival came suddenly alert. Shot, you damned fool, and you're lyin' here looking at the pretty clouds.

He got to his knees, his vision blurred, his shoulder numb, his blood racing. He could see the approaching rider now, a big man on a black horse, and he dived for his rifle, which lay nearby, thanking the fate that had given him old-time mountain men for teachers, the old-timers who hadn't believed in such tomfoolery as saddle boots for long guns, believed rather in keeping that rifle in your hands, inconvenient or not. "It's a hell of a lot more inconvenient to die," old Poke had said more than once.

The rifle lay there, cool and deadly, and Justice tried to dive for it. He tried, but shock was numbing his body and he lurched forward to land on his face, his outstretched fingers digging furrows in the earth as he clawed at it, hearing the drumming of approaching hoofbeats, the bellowing crash of another, nearer rifle shot.

Then his fingers found the Spencer and he managed to get to his knees, to brace himself, his hair hanging in his eyes, his finger slowly tightening around the curved steel trigger, and the .56 bucked against his shoulder.

He went down with a terrible scream, the black horse staggering to one side, then fleeing toward the west, and Ruff Justice, bracing himself with his rifle, got to his feet to stagger toward him.

Ruff stood there for a long while, swaying back and forth, looking down into the dead, brutal face of Jake Morgan. Ruff had finally met the old bull of the clan, and now the bull was dead. There were no more Morgans, would be none. Jake Morgan had come a long way to die and now he slept peacefully on the endless plains.

Ruff Justice looked to the skies, watching the clouds stack and drift, forming columns and towers, storybook figures against a brilliant blue sky. Then, shaking his head, he started off, walking heavily toward the sorrel horse, which stood watching, comprehending none of man's madness.

WESTWARD HO!

The following is the opening chapter from the next novel in the gun-blazing, action-packed new Ruff Justice series from Signet!

RUFF JUSTICE #14: THE STONE WARRIORS

"Bastards! Filthy bastards," Ansel Farmer hissed. They were still coming—the Stone Warriors. Farmer had shinnied up the wind-flagged red cedar to look back down their trail, a trail they had followed for day after interminable day through the Little Missouri badlands.

"Are they back there still?" Tom Keep called up. The man was ashen. The hole in his leg wasn't healing properly.

"Yes." Farmer hung his head with despair. They were there; they would always be there. Until they had killed every last one of Farmer's group.

"Oh, God!" Keep moaned, his features carved with anguish. He looked skyward into the brilliant Dakota sun. "Goddamn them! What do they want?"

The boy stood beside Keep. The kid was only sixteen, but he was taller than Keep, and now, as he placed an arm around the injured man, he appeared stronger and older.

Hell, Farmer thought with something approaching astonishment, he was stronger than Keep. Maybe stronger than Farmer himself. And that was something, when a man's son grew taller than he was, when he showed a strength sufficient to see him through in a man's world.

If his son, Andrew Jackson Farmer, ever got the chance to have a man's life.

Farmer looked out across the oak- and ash-stippled badlands again. He could see them distinctly. A patch of red and of blue—a blanket or a daubed war horse. They never got near enough for a rifle shot, however. Not for a good shot, though Farmer and his son, Keep, Dougherty, MacDonald, and Samuels had wasted a hundred rounds of ammunition on the Stone Warriors, trying to keep them off their back trail.

It hadn't worked worth a damn. They were still coming.

"Pa, we'd better get moving!"

"Yeah." Farmer started down the red cedar. He slipped, tore a gash in his forearm, and landed roughly. The boy helped him up.

"There many of them?" the kid wanted to know.

"Twelve. Same as always, Andy. Just the twelve of them."

"That can't be, Pa! I got one. I know I did. Day before yesterday. And MacDonald—he got one back at the crossing, remember?"

"They're still there, Andy. There's still twelve."

"For Christ's sake!" Tom Keep shouted. "Let's get moving."

"Take it easy, Tom."

Keep sat his horse unsteadily. Blood seeped through his pant leg, staining his jeans to a dark maroon. His face was waxen. He would never make it to Lode. Maybe none of them would.

There had been six of them, plus the old Arik, when they started. Now they were reduced to Farmer, the kid, and the badly wounded Tom Keep.

"We won't make it, Pa, not unless we unburden these animals. They're wore down."

Farmer looked at his own blue roan and nodded. The kid was right again. "Tom?"

"I'm damned if I'll leave my gold. Damned if I will! What's it all for, Ansel, if we get back without the gold?"

"It's the only way." Ansel Farmer nodded across the badlands. "They don't care about gold. Don't even know what it is, likely. Ignorant as can be."

"Then you leave your gold, Ansel Farmer. Damned if I will."

"Andy?"

"I already told you what I thought, Pa."

"Half of the gold's yours. Enough to get you started in anything you like."

"Won't do me no good dead," Andy said with a grin. Already he was untying the sacks of dust from his long-legged Appaloosa pony.

"Just hurry up," Keep said. He was clutching his leg with both hands. Blood continued to flow from it, to flow heavily.

Ansel Farmer and the boy hid their gold in a clump of yellow-gray boulders near a lightning-struck, ancient oak. Tom Keep didn't even watch them. His eyes were open, but he wasn't seeing much of anything.

"He won't be able to keep up with us, Pa," Andy Farmer whispered to his father as they crumbled broken rock into the narrow fissure where the eleven sacks of gold dust were hidden.

"No." Farmer shook his head. "He'll never make it with that load his horse is carrying."

"It's damned near murder to let him keep that gold with him."

"You want to take it away from him, son?"

"No." Andy Farmer looked at the wounded man, a man they had lived with, worked with, shared fire with for eight long months. "No, Pa. I couldn't do that."

"Nor could I."

Keep was looking at them now as they clambered down out of the rocks. The eyes were narrow, filled with pain and suspicion.

"Damnit," Keep hissed, "let's get moving, Ansel."

"Yes." Farmer looked down the long, white, flood-scoured gorge behind them. He couldn't see them now, but they were back there. They were Stone Warriors and they would not stop—nor could they be stopped.

That was what the old Arik had told them. "Nothing kills Stone Warriors. You are mad to go to their land to search for gold. All the men they see die. All the men. Ask those who know."

"Who are they?" Farmer had asked across the tiny fire, but the old Arik had shaken his head. He did not know.

"Sioux? Are they Sioux? Some ghost-dancer clan? Something like that?"

"Stone Warriors. If you go to their land you will not come back. No one will. Ask those who know."

But the Arik had agreed to be their guide into the badlands of western Dakota, to lead them into that tangle of gorges and gullies and weather-scoured hills along the Little Missouri. Three sacks of tobacco and a new Henry rifle had been enough to convince the old man.

Now he was dead. The Stone Warriors had done it. As they had killed Dougherty and MacDonald and Samuels.

The three rode up the long, dry canyon, the superheated wind moaning in the sparse stand of aspen—sere and gray compared to the high Colorado forests. That was Farmer's home, Colorado, and he longed for it now.

Keep's horse was lagging. They climbed a sandy draw and the animal sank to its knees. The burden was too much.

"Tom, you've got to unload."

"You go to hell!" the man flared up.

"You'll never keep up."

"Then go ahead without me—go ahead, damn you!"

The boy's eyes were on Farmer, questioning. Farmer shook his head. No, they couldn't leave him. Ansel looked back down the trail again, seeing nothing now but the dusty haze stirred up by the approaching riders. The bottom was soft; he couldn't hear their horses or see them. There was only the dust—and a knowledge beyond the senses.

"Damn you, Tom Keep," Farmer muttered. He swung down from his roan and got Keep's gelding by the bridle, leading it up out of the sandy wash. It stood quivering, foam flecking its flanks.

Ahead of them now the country flattened, smoothed, the long plains beginning. Dry yellow, endless, the Dakota prairie stretching out toward the Knife River and then the Missouri, Fort Lincoln and safety.

It was a long way, a hell of a long way.

The empty land passed beneath their horses' hooves; the sun was a white-hot hole in a blue-crystal sky burning shoulders and necks, blistering hands. Farmer's horse stumbled and he jerked its head up, cursing. The roan was weary as well. He patted the animal's neck, looking back across his shoulder, knowing what he would see, seeing it.

Dust rising in a thin, wind-twisted column.

"Why don't they quit! Why don't they give it up?" Anguish tugged down at the corners of Farmer's mouth. In anger, in frustration, he pulled his .44-40 Henry from his saddle boot and fired six rounds at the distant dust.

"Pa?"

The boy was looking at him oddly. Farmer could smell the gunsmoke, feel the hot metal in his hands. He wiped the sweat from his eyes and shook his head heavily.

"Why don't they leave us alone?"

"Come on, Pa."

They started again, riding eastward, always eastward across the unvarying plains, ignored by and ignoring in turn the scattered buffalo herds, the quick-leaping blur of pronghorn started into motion at their approach.

Keep's horse went down for good half an hour later. The gelding just folded up, unstrung. It went down hard on its neck, unseating Tom Keep, and it lay there, flanks heaving, eyes wide and showing much white.

"Get up, damn you!" Keep tried to yank it up by main strength, and when that failed, he began beating it with his rifle stock. Beating it savagely, brutally. It didn't matter—the horse was already dead.

"Come on, Tom. We've got to keep moving."

"Give me a hand with my dust."

"I'll take you up behind me, Tom, but I'm not taking your dust too."

"It's all I've got in the world!" Tom Keep shouted. He had his rifle in his hands still, and for a moment Andy Farmer thought he was going to turn the gun on them.

"Go on, then. . . . I'm not leaving it."

"Tom, be reasonable. . . .!"

"Pa, they're coming up a lot faster now."

"Tom!"

"Get out of here, you bastard!" Keep shouted, and Ansel Farmer just nodded, turning his roan eastward again. When he glanced back, Tom Keep was staggering after them, his gold-dust sacks tied together and slung over his neck.

"He'll never make it," Andy said. "He'll never make it an hour." There was no reply from his father.

They reached the Knife River in late afternoon. Cool, silver-blue, glistening in the sunlight. Andy Farmer swung down from his horse and stumbled to the river's edge to collapse on his belly against the sandy beach. Then he drank, drank until he was saturated with cool, clear water, until his belly was bloated and cramped with the drinking.

He sat up then, wiping back his blond hair, staring through the willows, in the direction they had come from. A lone crow sailed through an empty sky, calling. The land had gone suddenly still around him, and Andy didn't like the feel of it. He could no longer hear the cicadas, the frogs along the river.

"We've got to keep moving, Pa," he said, and the older man nodded heavily.

"Just a minute more." He sat on the sand, his head hanging. His horse drank and drank again. The water on its muzzle was like quicksilver in the sunlight when it lifted its head.

Something stark and cold reached out and ran fingers up Andy Farmer's spine. Tiny voices whispered mocking words in his ear.

"Pa!" The horse's head was lifting, turning as it looked with intensity toward the willows behind them. Its ears were pricked with curiosity, its eyes alert.

It saw, it heard, it knew. And so did Andy Farmer. He threw himself sharply to one side as the arrow flew past his face, burying itself in the sand. He grabbed at his holstered Remington pistol, firing three times into the willows, hitting nothing. He saw nothing, heard nothing. The horse yanked at the end of its tether, but Andy held it tight. His father's horse had gone galloping down the riverbank, stepping on its reins, tossing its head angrily.

"Pa!"

An arrow had gone all the way through Ansel Farmer's neck. Blood purpled the gray sand beneath him. Already the flies were coming.

"Pa?" Andy shook his father's shoulder, knowing it could do no good. Still he was unwilling to let him die, to admit that death could strike that close to him.

He drew away then, his teeth grinding together. He emptied his pistol into the willows, yanked his rifle from his saddle boot and emptied that as well.

The shots echoed away, smothered by the empty day. The river ran slowly into the distances.

Andrew Jackson Farmer, aged sixteen, swung up into the saddle and headed out across the Knife River, while behind him the Stone Warriors emerged from the brush to do their work on his father's body.

Reaching the far side, Andy rode into the brush, circled back toward the river, and got shakily down. He peered out across the mirror-bright river toward the far shore, knowing what he would see. The old Arik had told them what the Stone Warriors did to their enemies' bodies.

"Every bone. They must break every bone. Some say they do this so that the ghost cannot fight them again. They think they themselves come back from the grave. Maybe so," the old Indian had said, considering it thoughtfully.

Now Andy, his heart pumping wildly, watched them destroy his father's remains. Huge men, giants really, using logs and stones picked up along the river. He could see their arms raised overhead, hear the grunts of effort clearly as they smashed their tools down against Ansel Farmer's body.

They didn't speak; they never spoke, someone had said. They just battered the dead body, pulping and crushing it. Andy counted them. Twelve. His father had been right about that. There were still twelve of them—no matter that two of them had been killed back down the trail. . . . Andy wiped the sweat from his eyes and sighted down the long blue barrel of the Henry repeater he held.

He settled the bead sight into the notch, centered it on the heart of a Stone Warrior, and squeezed off.

Rapidly he levered in a fresh round, already knowing that the first shot had missed to the right. The thing turned slowly toward him, its mouth gaping open in a silent bellow, and Andy shot him again, seeing the Stone Warrior stagger backward as the .44-40 slug tagged him high on the chest.

The Stone Warriors ran to the willows where their horses were concealed, Andy's bullets pursuing them. A second warrior went down, pitching forward on his face to lie there unmoving.

"Two of them," Andy thought. "Two of the bastards."

He scrambled to his feet and leaped for his saddle, turning his horse out of there. The Stone Warriors were splashing across the river now, riding low across the withers of their ponies, waving their bows overhead.

Andy had a last glimpse of them before he reentered the willows and rode hell for it toward the open plains beyond. He had a last glimpse, and he counted them as they rode across the river, silent, implacable. There were twelve of them. Twelve. And not a sign of an injured man on the far bank. Only his father's broken, savaged body.

Andy felt the sob well up in his throat, a sob of futility and confusion. He looked at the Henry rifle in his hand, then flung it violently away, jamming his heels into the flanks of the big horse he rode.

Ahead lay the long plains, the distant Fort Lincoln, and maybe if a man rode far enough, fast enough, he could escape the death and the madness of the Stone Warriors.

JOIN THE RUFF JUSTICE READERS' PANEL

Help us bring you more of the books you like by filling out this survey and mailing it in today.

1. Book title:______________________________

   Book #:____________

2. Using the scale below how would you rate this book on the following features.

Poor		Not so Good		O.K.			Good		Excel-lent	
0	1	2	3	4	5	6	7	8	9	10

	Rating
Overall opinion of book	__________
Plot/Story	__________
Setting/Location	__________
Writing Style	__________
Character Development	__________
Conclusion/Ending	__________
Scene on Front Cover	__________

3. On average about how many western books do you buy for yourself each month?__________

4. How would you classify yourself as a reader of westerns?
   I am a ( ) light ( ) medium ( ) heavy reader.

5. What is your education?
   ( ) High School (or less) ( ) 4 yrs. college
   ( ) 2 yrs. college ( ) Post Graduate

6. Age________ 7. Sex: ( ) Male ( ) Female

Please Print Name______________________________

Address__________________________________

City______________State____________Zip________

Phone # ( )____________________

Thank you. Please send to New American Library, Research Dept, 1633 Broadway, New York, NY 10019.